Weedflower

cynthia kadohata

Atheneum Books for Young Readers
New York London Toronto Sydney

AUTHOR'S NOTE

This novel is based loosely on the internment of Japanese Americans in the Colorado River Relocation Center during World War II. Except for the end note, it is a work of fiction and should be viewed as such.

ATHENEUM BOOKS FOR YOUNG READERS• An imprint of Simon & Schuster Children's Publishing Division • 1230 Avenue of the Americas, New York, NY 10020 • This book is a work of fiction. Any references to historical events, real people, or real locales are used fictitiously. Other names, characters, places, and incidents are the product of the author's imagination, and any resemblance to actual events or locales or persons, living or dead, is entirely coincidental. • For information about special discounts for bulk purchases, please contact Simon & Schuster Special Sales at 1-866-506-1949 or business@simonandschuster.com. The Simon & Schuster Speakers Bureau can bring authors to your live event. For more information or to book an event contact the Simon & Schuster Speakers Bureau at 1-866-248-3049 or visit our website at www.simonspeakers.com. • Also available in a hardcover edition. • Book design by Ann Zeak • The text of this book was set in Berling. • Manufactured in the United States of America • 0611 OFF • First paperback edition January 2009 • 10 9 8 7 6 5 • The Library of Congress has cataloged the hardcover edition as follows: Kadohata, Cynthia. • Weedflower / Cynthia Kadohata. —1st ed. • p. cm. • Summary: After twelve-year-old Sumiko and her Japanese-American family are relocated from their flower farm in southern California to an internment camp on a Mojave Indian reservation in Arizona, she helps her family and neighbors, becomes friends with a local Indian boy, and tries to hold on to her dream of owning a flower shop. • ISBN 978-0-689-86574-9 (hc) • [1. Japanese Americans—Evacuation and relocation, 1942-1945. 2. World War, 1939-1945—United States—Juvenile fiction. 3. Mohave Indians—Juvenile fiction. 4. Indians of North America—Arizona—Juvenile fiction. 5. Arizona—History—1912-1950—Juvenile fiction 1950—Fiction. 6. Japanese Americans—Evacuation and relocation, 1942-1945—Fiction. 7. World War, 1939-1945—United States—Fiction. 8. Mohave Indians—Fiction. 9. Indians of North America—Arizona—Fiction. 10. Arizona—History—1912-1950—Fiction] • I. Title. • PZ7.K1166We 2006 • [Fic]—dc22 • 2004024912 • ISBN 978-1-4169-7566-3 (pbk)

For my father

Acknowledgments

Many people aided me in the writing of this novel—more people, I'm afraid, than I will be able to remember.

My friends George Miyamoto and Caitlyn Dlouhy sustained me in ways that I can only hope to repay.

And thanks to everyone at Atheneum, in particular Susan Burke, Ginee Seo, and Emma Dryden.

Donald H. Estes, Professor Emeritus of History at San Diego City College, read the manuscript twice, talked with me on the phone, provided much-needed advice and corrections, and tolerated it when I hounded him for help. I was also inspired and moved by "Hot Enough to Melt Iron: The San Diego *Nikkei* Experience 1942–1946" and "Further and Further Away—The Relocation of San Diego's *Nikkei* Community—1942," the articles cowritten by Professor Estes and his son, Matthew T. Estes. Professor Estes passed away in the spring of 2005.

A number of former internees, including Mas Inoshita, Tom Miyamoto, and Robert Wada, volunteered their time for interviews that provided many fascinating and particular details.

The Reverend Marvin Harada of the Orange County Buddhist Church set up interviews with former internees Harry Koide, Nami Okada, and Connie Shimojima.

Naomi Hirahara, author of *A Scent of Flowers: The History of the Southern California Flower Market, 1912–2004*; *Summer of the Big Bachi;* and other books, set up interviews with 1940s flower farmers Arthur Ito, Frank Kuwahara, Larry Nomura, Hideo "Jibo" Satow, and Mas Yoshida.

Former internee Ruth Okimoto spoke with me both about her experiences in camp and about her trenchant piece of research, *Sharing a Desert Home: Life on the Colorado River Indian Reservation*, which explores the relationship between the Japanese Americans incarcerated at Poston and the Native Americans living on the reservation. She also read the manuscript twice, for which I am eternally grateful, for in many ways this is *her* story.

Elders Gloria McVey, part Chemehuevi, and Henry Little,

Mojave, both grew up on the reservation and talked to me about life in those days before and during the war.

Endless thanks for the generosity and knowledge of Jay Cravath, PhD, of the Colorado River Indian Tribes Education Department. Dr. Cravath put me in touch with Gloria McVey and also found answers to many of my questions about life on the reservation during the war.

Reiko Lee generously read the whole manuscript and also consulted with her friend, the translator Yoshie Takahashi, to advise me on my Japanese usage. In addition Keith Holeman and Jeannette Miyamoto provided much invaluable advice on usage.

A tremendous resource for anyone studying the internment is the collection of interviews at the Center for Oral and Public History, California State University, Fullerton.

Dr. Kenneth William Townsend, author of *World War II and the American Indian*, advised me on the Poston section of the manuscript.

The amazing National Archives–Pacific Region (Laguan Niguel) holds many original documents pertaining to the Colorado River Relocation Center.

Many people took the time to answer my e-mailed queries, including Judy Hamaguchi of the Japanese American Historical Society, Karen Leong of Arizona State University, Teri Kuwahara of the Go For Broke Educational Foundation, and members of the IRRIGATION-L.org listserv. I'd also like to thank RJ Long, Donald Coffin, Charles Wiggins, C. J. Hobijn, and some other members of the greyhoundthroughexpress Yahoo group, although the lengthy section about a bus trip was cut from the final manuscript.

I am profoundly grateful and fortunate.

1

THIS IS WHAT IT FELT LIKE TO BE LONELY:

1. Like everyone was looking at you. Sumiko felt this once in a while.
2. Like *nobody* was looking at you. Sumiko felt this a lot.
3. Like you didn't care about anything at all. She felt this maybe once a week.
4. Like you were *just* about to cry over every little thing. She felt this about once daily.

But not today! Sumiko jumped off the school bus and ran behind her house. Her family was working;

she saw their small forms surrounded by bursts of color in the flower fields. "Jiichan!" she shouted to her grandfather. She waved an envelope at him. "I'm invited to a party!"

"Can't hear!"

"I'm invited to a party!"

Everybody was looking at her, but nobody seemed to understand what she was saying. Oh, forget it! She ran into the stable to look for her little brother, Tak-Tak, but he wasn't there. Baba just looked at her expectantly. She patted the old nag's yellow nose and said, "I'm invited to a party." Baba didn't change expressions.

She hurried inside the house to change into her work clothes. That morning Sumiko and some other kids in her sixth-grade class had received invitations to a birthday party this Saturday. One of the popular girls was holding a party and had decided at the last minute to invite everyone in the class. The invitation was embossed, and the lettering inside was gold. Sumiko had read the inside about a dozen times:

We are pleased to invite you
to a birthday party for
Marsha Melrose
12372 La Mirada Terrace
Saturday, December 6, 1941
1–3 p.m.

The invitation reminded Sumiko of the expensive valentines her cousin Ichiro gave to girls he especially liked.

She changed clothes behind the blankets her aunt and uncle had strung across the bedroom. She shared the room with Takao, a.k.a. Tak-Tak. Auntie and Uncle had strung the blankets up three weeks earlier when Sumiko turned twelve. She felt guilty because she actually liked the blankets, even though Tak-Tak had cried over them. He was almost six and he followed her around day and night. She loved him like crazy. But she still liked the blankets.

Sumiko stuck the invitation into her shirt pocket so that she could look at it now and then while she worked. This was the first class party she'd ever been invited to.

Through a fluke, Sumiko lived in a school district with few Japanese. She was the only Japanese girl in her class, whereas if she'd lived a few miles away, several Japanese girls would have been in the same class. The white girls were nice enough to her during recess, but she had never been invited to play on weekends or sleep over at anyone's house or anything like that.

She didn't used to worry about it as much as she did lately. The way Jiichan told the story, Sumiko had been born cheerful, had become sad when her parents died when Tak-Tak was a baby, had begun to get cheerful again, and now was just "starting to act like a female." He'd said that because she had asked for a mirror for her bureau so she could decide when it was time to start curling her long hair. Instead of a mirror, she'd gotten the blankets.

"Hurry!" Tak-Tak called out. "Or we won't have time to brush Baba."

She stepped around the blanket divider and saw that her brother had come in. "I'm invited to a party." She waved the invitation at him.

He looked at her blankly. He wore black-framed glasses that stayed attached to his head with an elastic band Auntie had made. The lenses were so thick, his eyes always looked big.

Tak-Tak clearly didn't understand the significance of her invitation. Finally he said, "We have to brush Baba. You promised me before you went to school."

He looked a little forlorn over the thought that she might have forgotten what she promised him. "Did you clean Baba's brush?" she asked.

He held up a clean horse brush. "I'll race you!"

She let Tak-Tak stay one step ahead of her as they ran outside to the stable. "You beat me!" she cried as they fell into some hay.

Sumiko smiled as Tak-Tak jumped up from the hay to brush the horse. Tak-Tak really adored Baba. Her nose dripped all the time, but that worked out fine because Tak-Tak liked gooey things. Sumiko sat up and looked out the stable door. Her cousins Bull and Ichiro were still tending the flowers, nineteen-year-old Bull wide and strong and twenty-three-year-old Ichiro slender and lean, graceful even in his farm clothes. Uncle was working at the far end of the fields among the carnations, which he always liked to take care of himself. The carnations grew in a makeshift, open-field greenhouse, where they were protected from extremes of sun or wind. Uncle was cutting some for tomorrow's wholesale flower market. Ichiro and Bull were pulling weeds among the stock. Local flower farmers called flowers grown in the field *kusabana*—"weedflowers." Stock were weedflowers that emanated an amazing clovelike fragrance. Of all the flowers her family had ever grown, Sumiko loved them most.

Ragged white cheesecloth rippled above parts of the fields. Last spring Sumiko and Auntie had sewn cheesecloth tarps for the men to hang over the fields to protect the flowers—except the stock, which didn't need protection.

Uncle dreamed of setting up a glass greenhouse someday and growing perfect carnations, but so far that was just talk. Only the wealthier Japanese farmers owned glass greenhouses. Uncle said you could control the elements better with a greenhouse. Perfection was the Holy Grail to Uncle. Sumiko thought that a lot of the flowers were perfect, but Uncle often looked critically at his carnations and said things like, "They would be perfect if we had a glass greenhouse." He never even considered whether the stock could reach perfection—after all, they were just weedflowers.

Most of the greenhouse growers came from families who'd moved to America before laws were passed preventing those born in Asia from becoming citizens. Uncle and Jiichan had both been born in Japan. People born in Asia were not allowed to become American citizens, and those who weren't citizens were not allowed to own or lease land. Because her cousin Ichiro was born in the United States, the farm's lease was in his name instead of his father's.

Sumiko turned her attention back to the stable to check on her brother. Tak-Tak had climbed a stool and was brushing Baba's mane. Tak-Tak loved Sumiko best of anything in the world. But Sumiko thought maybe he loved the horse second best.

Now she saw her grandfather walk into the outhouse. That was always the first thing he did when he finished working. "I have to start the bathwater," she told Tak-Tak, who barely noticed as she hurried away. In the bathhouse she got kindling from a pile and placed it under the big tub. She lugged a few logs off the woodpile and placed them atop the kindling and started a fire. As soon as the bathwater started steaming, she would place a wooden platform in the tub so the bottom wouldn't be too hot to step in.

"Sumiko-chan!" her grandfather called from the outhouse. There was a crack in the wood that he always peered out of. Sometimes he liked to talk to the family right through the outhouse wall! He had no dignity because he was so old. Still, he made Sumiko smile a lot. She ran to the outhouse.

"Yes, Jiichan."

"When is party?" he said.

"I thought you didn't hear me."

"Whole neighborhood hear you," he said.

"It's Saturday."

He didn't speak. Sometimes he just stopped talking, and you didn't know whether you were supposed to wait at the outhouse or not. If you asked him if he wanted you to wait outside, he would snap that you had interrupted his train of thought. If you waited without asking, he would look surprised when he came out.

"I thinking, maybe it better I drive you to party instead of your uncle," he suddenly said. "I wait in car nearby in case you get hurt." Though Jiichan had lived in the United States for several decades, he didn't sound like it. Sometimes he spoke *chanpon*, which was a mix of Japanese and English; sometimes he spoke Japanese; and when he talked to Sumiko and Tak-Tak, he spoke mangled English.

Jiichan already seemed as obsessed with this party as Sumiko was.

"Jiichan! I'm not going to get hurt at a birthday party!" she said to the outhouse.

"I just thinking. But if you got no respect for old man opinion, never mind, never mind."

Sumiko laughed. "I'm going to be fine. Maybe they'll ask me to sing a song!" Was that what they did at birthday parties? She liked to sing. Once she'd even been chosen to sing a song alone during a school assembly. She'd gotten a little flustered and sung the same verse twice, but otherwise, she'd done great. She imagined a crowd of classmates surrounding her at the party.

"Sumiko!" Jiichan said. "Are you listening?"

"Sorry, Jiichan. What did you say?"

"I say go get your uncle!"

She shouted out, "Uncle! Jiichan wants you!" Uncle looked up from the fields and headed in.

"You break my eardrum," Jiichan said.

Sumiko returned to the bathhouse to check the water (not hot enough yet), went into the stable to check Tak-Tak (still brushing Baba), and hurried to the shed to grade the cut carnations Ichiro had just brought in from the field. He smiled as she passed.

The shed was yet another drafty building on the farm. Empty *taru*—barrels—that soy sauce came in were piled on top of one another along the walls, waiting to be filled with carnations for tomorrow morning's market. Sumiko was supposed to grade the flowers and put them into the *taru*. That was one of her main jobs.

Flower farmers charged more for their most beautiful, biggest, nearly flawless flowers. Sumiko graded the best carnations #1 and the next best #2. Only carnations were graded inside the shed. The stock were graded right out in the field.

The worst carnations that farmers sold were splits—flowers where the calyx didn't hold the petals together right. They were still pretty, but they were bought by funeral parlors or else cheap markets like street-corner flower vendors. Jiichan said men bought street-corner flowers on the way home from work on days when their wives were mad at them. He said someday he was going to write a book of all his theories.

Sometimes Sumiko slipped a #1 flower into the splits because she felt sorry for the poor dead people who were getting defective flowers. But she also felt guilty that a good flower might be wasted on dead people who wouldn't even notice. So either way she felt a little bad.

As she picked up the first stem from the pile, Sumiko remembered proudly how Uncle had said she was the only one in the family whose hands were both quick and gentle—perfect hands for grading. In fact, she was the only one in the family allowed to grade the carnations. That was one reason she knew how important she was to the farm. From the beginning, Uncle and Auntie had never asked her to work, but she still remembered lying in her new bedroom after her parents died, worrying that she and her brother would get sent to an orphanage. So the next day she'd gotten up and scrubbed all the floors. Jiichan still brought it up sometimes. "I remember when your parents die, all you do is scrub floor for week. We thought you crazy." And she had not stopped working since then.

She placed a batch of #1s into the *taru*. Tak-Tak came in and watched her for a moment. "Do you think Baba loves me or Bull or you more?" he asked.

"Maybe she loves all of us for different reasons."

"Why does she love me?"

"Because you brush her." He was silent, and she glanced at him. He was smiling to himself. Then his eyes grew curious. "Why does she love Bull?" he said.

"Because he was her first friend."

"Does she love you?"

"Yes, because I'm her friend too."

He followed her to the bathhouse to put the platform in the bottom of the tub, and then he followed her back to the shed.

Sumiko separated some of the bunches by color but mixed the colors in other bunches. Sometimes she took too long to bunch flowers because she liked them to look just so. Personally, she didn't favor the reds, pinks, and whites of carnations. She liked the stock better—they came in just about every color. Lately, peach was her favorite stock color. In fact, she'd made Uncle plant a little section of just peach so that she could use the flowers for the dinner table.

She kept the shed door open so she could keep track of who was walking in and out of the bathhouse. The men bathed in order of age—Jiichan first, then Uncle, then Ichiro, then Bull, and then Tak-Tak. After that came Auntie and, finally, Sumiko. Every night while Tak-Tak took his bath, Sumiko went inside the house to start the rice. She always divided daytime and nighttime by when Tak-Tak finished his bath. After he finished bathing, it was considered nighttime, and just a few mealtime chores remained before Sumiko allowed herself to stop working.

Tonight she couldn't wait until dinner was over so she could take the time to study her two best dresses and decide what to wear to the party. Auntie had made her a new dress a few months ago for a wedding. The dress actually rustled when she walked! She also owned a mint green school dress that she liked. It was a hard decision.

2

WHEN AUNTIE FINISHED BATHING, SUMIKO WENT OUT for her turn. To keep the water clean for as many days as possible, they all washed themselves off with sponges, soap, and a bucket of water before they got into the tub. By the time Sumiko bathed, both the water and the air had cooled off. Sumiko could not remember ever taking a hot bath in a nice steamy room.

She got undressed and sponged off. She always checked the scars on her tummy, from the car accident her parents had been killed in so many years earlier. She didn't remember much about it except spinning around.

She climbed into the tub and swooshed her whole head and body under the water. The water pressed softly against her face. She had a thought and sat up quickly. Should she bring some flowers to the party? Someday when she achieved her goal of owning a flower shop, she would be an expert in arranging flowers. She loved to create arrangements for the dining-room table. Sometimes she liked an orderly arrangement, and sometimes she liked something wilder. Now she decided to bring a bunch of peach stock to the party. Everyone would love the scent and the wildness of the flowers.

She held her breath and dunked underneath the water again. When she lifted her head, she could feel a breeze from a crack in the wall. She stepped into the chilly air, dried off quickly, and went inside without draining the tub. It was her job to decide when to empty the tub and put in fresh water. Auntie didn't like to waste water, so sometimes Sumiko kept the same water all week. On the farm they all had their farm duties, and in general they didn't like to tell one another how to do their jobs. Once in a while someone would say casually within her hearing, "The bathwater is getting a little stale." Or, "I wonder when Sumiko will change the bathwater." Today the water was definitely getting a little musty, but not quite musty enough to change.

That night Sumiko couldn't focus on any of

the chatter during dinner. The grown-ups seemed obsessed with someone named Mrs. Sumiko Hata, whose brother and husband had suffered heart attacks within days of each other, which resulted in Mrs. Hata's son taking over their Oregon potato farm, which started a chain reaction that ended in the previously wealthy Hata family nearly going broke and thereby providing gossip for *Nikkei* all up and down the coast. *Nikkei* were anyone in America of Japanese descent, whether they were born in the United States or Japan. Sumiko had never met Mrs. Hata, and neither had her family.

Jiichan liked to say that Sumiko's head was divided in half: the half that liked to work and the half that liked to daydream. As everyone ate and chatted she started daydreaming about what kind of cake Marsha Melrose would serve at her party. Sumiko's most favorite cake ever was the strawberry cake that Mrs. Muramoto had served one year at the Muramotos' annual New Year's Day party. If Marsha's mother served strawberry cake, she wasn't sure whether it would be considered rude to ask for a second slice. Her mind snapped back to the table when she heard Ichiro say, "A friend of mine thinks that the U.S. government may execute all the *Nikkei* if war with Japan breaks out."

Sumiko had heard that rumor before, but Uncle had admonished her not to believe it. He said "only crazy people" believed that. Still, she couldn't stop herself from asking, "Which friend?" Some of Ichiro's friends had been to college, so they were really smart.

Ichiro started to answer, but Auntie cut him off. "No war talk at the dinner table."

It was all really complicated, and things changed constantly. But as far as Sumiko understood, Nazi Germany had taken over France, Yugoslavia, Greece, Austria, and some other countries, and Germany had bombed England and then attacked the Soviet Union, or else attacked the Soviet Union and *then* bombed England . . . or maybe did them both at once. And Ichiro said the United States had imposed an oil embargo on Japan, who had signed a pact with Germany and Italy. And this was all just off the top of Sumiko's head—there was a lot more going on. The world was a huge mess. But the United States was officially neutral, and Ichiro had read somewhere that more than 90 percent of Americans opposed getting involved in the war. So Sumiko assumed there would be no war and she could continue to work on her flowers until things settled down.

Every day she looked at the peaceful flower fields, and sat in school learning social studies and math and music, and slept in her warm bed, and she just couldn't believe that the United States would ever get involved in a war.

Ichiro looked at his watch. He went out a lot, but Auntie always insisted he stay until dinner was finished.

Ichiro was a dandy. He'd already gotten ready to go out, which meant he'd smeared grease through his hair. Sumiko could smell it from where she was sitting across the table. And he was actually wearing gold suspenders a girlfriend had made him. Tee-hee! He liked girls and gambling, and he spent a lot of his money on clothes. Sumiko couldn't imagine why girls would like gold suspenders and greasy hair; still, she had to admit it suited Ichiro. But he was just as handsome in overalls.

Bull's hair was a *big* mess, like it always was after his bath. Before his bath his hair was usually a *small* mess. He did try to comb it in the mornings, but the combing didn't "take" because his hair was bristly as a horse brush.

Sumiko often marveled over how different Ichiro and Bull were. Bull didn't even pick out his own clothes—Auntie made him overalls and shirts. He rarely went out for fun except when he played baseball with other *Nikkei*. He did have a girlfriend a couple of years ago, but Sumiko didn't know what had become of that. Ichiro, on the other hand, went out with girls all the time. But the point was, Ichiro knew a lot of people and heard all the important rumors.

One "rumor" that was not a rumor: Last August a U.S. congressman had suggested that ten thousand Japanese Americans ought to be incarcerated and held as hostages to make sure Japan would not act in a hostile manner toward the United States. Sumiko remembered when they'd all heard that on the radio. Auntie had exclaimed, "Law-abiding citizens held hostage!" The grown-ups had discussed that for weeks. Sumiko did not believe it was possible. White people treated her fairly enough. In fact, there was a lady at the grocery store who gave her a free apple once.

Sumiko swallowed some rice. "A white lady gave me an apple once," she said.

Everybody just looked at her uncomprehendingly.

"Mother, I need to get going," Ichiro said.

Auntie said, "We're almost finished."

They frowned at each other.

Jiichan took out his teeth and looked at them and put them back in. Sumiko moved her eyes to Auntie to see her reaction. Auntie laid the palm of her right hand softly against her heart, as if she were having a mild attack.

Jiichan didn't notice. He went back to attacking his food, slurping a piece of meat into his mouth as if it were a noodle. Jiichan's lean face fascinated Sumiko. If she hadn't known him, she would think he was angry all the time. His cheekbones jutted out, and he scowled even when he was joking. He'd come to America because he was a second son. Among the Japanese, a father left everything he owned to his first son. So Jiichan had always struggled for money, and some people thought he was bitter. But Sumiko was glad he was a second son, because otherwise, he never would have come to America and she and Tak-Tak would have been born in Japan.

Now he took out his teeth again and studied them as if they were a crystal ball. "Someday Bull be as strong as I once was," he predicted. He put his teeth back in.

Sumiko and Tak-Tak giggled. Food splattered out of Tak-Tak's mouth as he tried to hold back full laughter.

Auntie looked at Uncle, which meant that Uncle was supposed to say something. Uncle finally came up with, "Children, no giggling at the table."

Auntie frowned at Tak-Tak, and Jiichan frowned at Auntie.

Uncle and Auntie were in their late forties, and their faces were lined and dark from working in the fields all their lives. But Uncle smiled more than Auntie. Auntie did not have a sense of humor, or at least that's what Jiichan said when they were cross with each other one day.

All during dinner Sumiko's legs swung and shook

with impatience. She wanted to finish so she could study her dresses. Toward the end of dinner even Auntie seemed impatient. The whole family watched Jiichan chew slowly. Dinner was never over until he stopped chewing. Every time he seemed about to stop, he would frown thoughtfully at the table and refill his plate. Finally he frowned thoughtfully at the table . . . and didn't fill his plate! He pushed his chair back and looked warningly at everyone. "Need digestive peace now." He ambled away, no doubt to sit in his chair and digest.

After Sumiko washed the dishes, she rushed to her bedroom so she could study her dresses. Her crisp blue dress had been worn only once. But her mint green school dress was her favorite dress ever. And once when she was wearing it, the boy who worked at the grocery store had said it was pretty. She pulled the blanket divider closed so she could think about the dresses in private. If she'd had a mirror, she would have tried them on.

But when she heard Tak-Tak climb into his bed, she went around to tuck him in. He lay in bed with his glasses on and his cage of pet crickets on his pillow.

"Can I take off your glasses?" she said.

"But what if I get up in the middle of the night and can't see anything?" That was a big fear of his lately.

"I'll be right here."

"Okay," he said reluctantly.

He sat up, and she took off his glasses. Whenever she took them off, a ridge from the band jutted out from his hair.

"I'm putting them right here on the nightstand," she said.

"Uh-huh." He pulled his blanket over his head without saying good night.

"Do you want me to put the crickets on the table?"

"Okay."

She set the cage on the table. "They're right here," she said. He didn't answer.

Sumiko turned off his light. Then, after she got in bed, he called out to her, "Do you think they'll kill us if war breaks out?" His voice was muffled, so she knew he still lay under his blanket.

"Uncle will protect us."

"Are you sure?"

"Yes."

And she was sure. She'd heard similar rumors for almost as long as she could remember. She trusted Uncle a lot. He wouldn't let anything happen to them.

Sumiko looked out the window. In the fields the tattered pieces of cheesecloth rippled like ghosts. Far away she could see the flower fields of their neighbors Mr. and Mrs. Ono. Mr. Ono believed in the future, and he liked to say that inventions were the foundation of the future. His own newest invention: lights he'd hung over his fields to try to force some chrysanthemums to bloom early. Other farmers used lights too, but he said his lights were special. He also had developed a special strain of chrysanthemums that was much in demand at the market.

The lights twinkled like low-hanging stars above his fields. A few years ago he had tried to keep his fields warm in the winter by burning tires. The smell reached all the way to Sumiko's house. Her family had needed to keep their windows closed the whole winter. Now Sumiko opened the windows to let the cool December air waft into the room.

Tak-Tak's pet crickets chirped loudly, a sound Sumiko loved since crickets were good luck. The chirping seemed farther away than usual. Sumiko's mind was already drifting to thoughts of Saturday's party. The party was the only thing that seemed real. Marsha Melrose wasn't the most popular girl in class, but she was definitely popular. Sumiko could already imagine Marsha's house and how beautiful it would be. Marsha's father was a city councilman, and her mother was a real, true ex-ballerina. Originally, the Melrose fortune had come from a magic elixir that Marsha's great-grandfather had invented during the pioneer days. Jiichan said it was not elixir, but "a bunch of crock." Only he pronounced it more like "clock." Sumiko lay back and pulled her blanket around her.

The crickets chirped and chirped.

3

Before breakfast the next morning Sumiko put on two sweaters over her work clothes and went out to disbud the carnations. The carnations and stock emitted a similar scent. In the mornings the air was thick with it. Sumiko blew on her hands to warm them. Everyone else was already working.

Disbudding was women's work—on a couple of occasions when Sumiko was sick, her uncle had hired local girls to disbud. Later she'd felt a little jealous when he'd said they did a good job. But then he'd told her that she worked faster than the other girls. Disbudding required quick judgment, because you needed to decide which bud was the strongest on a plant. You pinched or clipped off the weakest buds in favor of the one strong bud, so as to end up with one beautiful, strong flower. Sumiko used a special knife that she'd gotten for Christmas last year. Every year at least one person in Sumiko's class asked her, "Are you Buddhist? Do you celebrate Christmas?" Sumiko was Buddhist, but actually, every Buddhist she knew celebrated Christmas by getting a tree and giving gifts.

Uncle had painted the handle of her knife yellow and then had painted SUMIKO'S PROPERTY on one side of the handle and DO NOT TOUCH on the other. She always cleaned and sharpened her knife after she disbudded.

She moved quickly down the row of flowers. Every so often she spotted a flower and just *knew* it would be the best flower. Other times she needed to make a quick decision about which would be the best. She liked how she needed to work and think at the same time to be a really good disbudder.

Auntie called out, "You'll miss the school bus!"

Sumiko jumped up without finishing the row, because Auntie got irate when Sumiko missed the bus and had to be driven to school by a neighbor.

She just managed to change clothes, grab her books, and run like mad to the road before the bus braked to a stop at her house. Sumiko preferred to sit at the front of the school bus. Sometimes some of the boys taunted her for being Japanese, but if she sat in front, they didn't bother her unless they were in a mean mood. Today she sat right near the driver. Her stomach gurgled in hunger because she hadn't had time to eat breakfast. She looked out the window. A few of the flower growers also grew vegetables. Before her parents had died, they had leased a celery farm twenty miles away, but she couldn't remember any of that no matter how hard she tried.

"Sumiko!"

Sumiko jumped to her feet. "Yes, Mr. Johnson."

"I said, name a major export of the West Indies."

West Indies! Sumiko had thought the class was discussing India, not the Indies. She'd been thinking about the party again and about how she hoped she would remember enough details about it to satisfy her family. She glanced down at her book. She wasn't even on the page about India, but about Venezuela. She blurted out, "Tractors!"

Mr. Johnson looked pained. He rubbed both sides of his forehead with his palms. It wasn't personal; he did things like that whenever anyone got a wrong answer. Tractors—what had she been thinking? She felt her face grow hot.

Sometimes Mr. Johnson took out his handkerchief and wiped his eyes as if he were crying. Now he shook his head sadly and walked to the blackboard and wrote *Sumiko—P*. They were playing P-I-G. Mr. Johnson asked everybody geography questions, and then every time a student got a wrong answer, the student got a letter. The first one to get "P-I-G" was the loser. Everyone got to call the loser "pig" all day.

Sumiko sat down.

"Susan, name a major export of the West Indies."

Susan jumped up. "Bananas, Mr. Johnson." Susan smiled and sat down. Susan was one of Marsha's best friends. Neither of them had ever been "P-I-G." Neither had Sumiko, but she'd gotten "P-I" twice. During class she often found herself worrying about the farm. Once after a strong wind some of the cheesecloth had fallen down and crushed the carnations. Another time Tak-Tak got stung by a wasp, and first his arm and then his head swelled up. Sumiko wasn't there, but Uncle had described it in detail because he knew Sumiko would want to know exactly what had happened. She liked to know every important thing that happened to Tak-Tak and every important thing that happened on the farm.

Now, she was thinking about how Uncle had told her he would buy a present for Marsha on the way home from the flower market.

"Sumiko!" shouted Mr. Johnson. She jumped to her feet again. She knew it was her lucky day because Mr. Johnson said, "Name a major export of Venezuela!"

She glanced down at her book and then said, "Oil." She sat down happily.

The school bus passed a bunch of *Nikkei* kids on bicycles. They were probably headed for Japanese school. Sumiko didn't attend Japanese school after regular school because her family needed her too much on the farm. They'd tried sending her to Japanese school for a while, but she'd ended up falling behind in her regular school. Sometimes she thought she might have more friends if she attended Japanese school.

The bus passed Nori Muramoto on his shiny bike. He got a new one every year. His father owned a carnation empire. Once Nori had called her "Weedflower," like an insult. She'd called him "Uglybrain" and gotten grounded for a week. She never went anywhere anyway, so getting grounded didn't affect her much.

On Friday after school the bathwater was "ripe," to use Auntie's word. But Sumiko didn't drain it because on Saturday, Bull was going to break up horse manure for fertilizer, and she would drain the water after he washed up from that. Bull had manure duty because he was the youngest working male. When Tak-Tak was a few years older, he would have to spread the manure. Sumiko and Auntie never bathed on the days the manure was spread because no matter how well Bull sponged off beforehand, the water still stank after his bath. Tak-Tak bathed anyway. He loved the smell. Sometimes when Sumiko lay in bed making up lists before she went to sleep, she thought of Tak-Tak's four favorite things or animals:

1. Baba
2. Crickets
3. Goo
4. Bad smells

That evening they waited fifteen minutes at the dinner table for Uncle to appear. He finally hurried in—his face shining—from his special room in the shed. Nobody was allowed in his special room. Uncle was trying to develop new strains of carnations and stock in there. Jiichan liked to joke that Uncle was a mad scientist.

"I think I've almost got it," Uncle said. "We're going to have the best carnations in Southern California."

Auntie frowned. "You're late for dinner." She began spooning rice into his bowl and mumbling, "Best, second best, what's the difference? How can a flower be best?" She gasped as her eyes fell on Uncle's hands. "Look at those nails! At my dinner table!"

Sumiko noticed Bull and Ichiro immediately slip their hands underneath the table. Uncle looked like Tak-Tak getting caught doing something he shouldn't. Auntie shooed Uncle away to clean his nails. Jiichan laid his hands on the table, as if daring Auntie to say something to him. She didn't.

Uncle returned from the kitchen and immediately began eating. At dinner each Friday, Uncle liked them all to tell of anything special on their minds. When it was Sumiko's turn, she planned to talk about the party. "Why don't you start this week?" Uncle said to Tak-Tak. "What's on your mind?"

"Are they going to kill us?" Tak-Tak asked.

Uncle set down his chopsticks and leaned forward. "Nobody's going to kill us."

Jiichan tapped Tak-Tak's arm as if knocking on a door. "I beat up anyone who try! I beat up three man once!"

Auntie frowned at Sumiko. "Aren't you taking care of your brother?"

"I am!" Sumiko said. "I told him nobody is going to kill us!" But Auntie had already looked away.

Uncle said, "Bull, anything on your mind this week?"

Sumiko waited. She knew Bull would say something about the flowers.

Bull said, "We ran out of nicotine." Most of the flower farmers used nicotine as a pesticide. Bull knew everything about the farm. He knew big facts, like how many acres of which flower they'd planted in what year; and he knew little facts, like where Sumiko had left her knife the only time she'd ever mislaid it.

Ichiro yawned, and as he so often did, he glanced ostentatiously at his watch.

Tak-Tak persisted. "But what if they kill us? My friend Isamu's father said they might."

Sumiko gently shushed him. She picked rice off his shirt. "You have *gohan* all over you." She snapped his glasses band, but he didn't think that was funny.

Uncle said again, "Nobody's going to kill anybody."

Still, Sumiko noticed that Uncle and Auntie met eyes over the table, and Auntie pressed her lips together.

She saw that Tak-Tak noticed as well. So she said, "Tak-Tak, do you want to play cards before you go to sleep?"

"Yes!"

"We'll play *hanafuda*." *Hanafuda* was played with a special deck of cards, each card with a picture of a flower on it. Sumiko and her brother played a game they made up. Sometimes she invented new rules as they went along so that Tak-Tak could win.

Ichiro laughed. "That old-man game!"

"Old man!" said Jiichan. "Someday you be old man! I beat up three man at same time when I was young!"

Conversations with Jiichan often traveled in a circle and sometimes in a figure eight. You started out one place, and you ended up in the same place.

The rest of the dinnertime conversation was small

talk. Tak-Tak's question had distracted everybody, and Uncle had never gotten around to asking the rest of them what was on their minds. Uncle was chattering about baseball. Sumiko was never going to get her turn to speak! Finally she exploded: "Uncle, did you get the present?"

"Get what present?"

She cried out, "Did you forget? I—" She stopped in midsentence. She noticed his lips quivering and his eyes starting to shine. How could he joke about something this important?

"Let's see, where did I put it?" He pushed out from his chair and rummaged through the bureau. "I hope I can find it. Ah, here it is." He opened up a box and pulled out an exquisite silk flowered scarf. "Those flowers are birds of paradise," he said.

She jumped up. "Uncle, it's *beautiful.*" She reached out but then decided not to touch it.

"How much was it?" said Auntie.

Uncle didn't meet Auntie's eyes as he mumbled, "Four dollars."

"Four dollars!" Auntie clutched at her chest.

Four dollars! That was more than a day's wages for some men. Sumiko felt guilty, and ecstatic, and guilty, and ecstatic.

After dinner Auntie helped her wrap the scarf. Three times she muttered, "Four dollars," and Sumiko felt guilty again.

After a game of cards with Tak-Tak, Sumiko checked her dresses once more and decided to wear the rustly blue one. Then she checked the wrapped present, which was beautiful and elegant in pink. Someday she would make the price up to Uncle.

4

"CAN I WALK BY MYSELF?" SUMIKO, UNCLE, AND JIICHAN sat in the truck, down the street from Marsha's house where she'd made Uncle stop. She was ashamed of herself, but she didn't want anyone to see the old truck.

Jiichan said, "You ashamed of family? Shame on you!"

"No, Jiichan, I just . . ."

Uncle chimed in: "She just wants to show she's a big girl."

"Not big enough to drive to party by self," Jiichan muttered. But he seemed resigned, and Sumiko got ready to jump from the truck.

"Okay, I'll be back right here for you in two hours," Uncle said.

She reached across Jiichan and hugged Uncle wildly. "I love you, Uncle!"

He beamed at her. She ran off even though she heard Jiichan complaining, "No hug for old man!"

Her blue dress rustled as she stepped onto the street. She waited until the old truck had gone before walking to Marsha's house and up the porch steps. She could hear music already: Glenn Miller, one of Auntie's radio favorites. And so many voices! It was a boy-girl party, the first anyone in her class had ever thrown. She breathed deeply of the scent from her beautiful bunch of peach stock. She made herself stop smiling so she would seem gracious instead of silly when the door opened. Then she knocked firmly on the door.

A maid opened up. The maid looked surprised to see Sumiko but took her present and flowers. The first thing that caught Sumiko's eyes was a large painting of whom she assumed was Marsha's mother in a tutu. The painting was so beautiful, Sumiko felt breathless. Then something kind of rolled across the room, but she wasn't sure what it was. Then she realized it was silence. She'd once seen a short film clip of time-lapse photography, of shadow moving across a field. That was the way the silence rolled across the room, starting at the far side and ending right here, with her.

Across the room Marsha's mother, Mrs. Melrose, was staring right at Sumiko. She looked just like the painting. Her lips were coral, and her dress was royal blue. Sumiko checked to make sure nobody else was nearby whom Mrs. Melrose might be looking at. No, it was just her. Mrs. Melrose smiled and moved gracefully across the room. She put out her hand. "I'm Marsha's mother," she said. The room grew loud again.

Sumiko smiled with relief and shook the lovely hand that was offered. She gushed, "Your house is beautiful!" She'd scarcely had a chance to see the house, but she'd noticed the couch was velvet and the ceilings were high and the doorways were arched. The boys wore neckties, the girls colorful dresses. Marsha's mother put an arm around Sumiko and moved her onto the front porch.

In the sunlight Mrs. Melrose looked older than she had inside. But her eyes were kind. She smiled so warmly that Sumiko couldn't help smiling even harder than she already was. Mrs. Melrose shut the door gently behind them. Sumiko thought Mrs. Melrose wasn't so much graceful as she was elegant. She wore a diamond clip in her hair! It was shaped like a slice of melon and must have had thirty diamonds in it.

"Marsha didn't tell me you were in her class."

"Oh, I've been in her class since she moved into the district."

"It's just . . . she had mentioned there was a Japanese girl at her school, but I didn't know she meant in her class. So when she asked whether she could invite the whole class, naturally I said yes."

Sumiko didn't understand. "Yes, I think every single person said they were coming. Marsha did a poll on Friday."

Marsha's mother touched her face and said in a soothing voice, "What lovely skin you have."

"Thank you!"

Mrs. Melrose smiled again. "It's not me, dear, but my husband has a few friends in back, some of the other parents who helped him raise some money for a charity we work with." She looked hopeful, as if she wanted something from Sumiko. "I just want you to understand that if it were up to me . . ."

And Sumiko realized that she was being uninvited. Marsha's mother saw that she understood and said, "Wait here." She went inside, again gently closing the door, and in a moment she reappeared with a big slice of chocolate cake on a cloth napkin. "You can keep the napkin!" she said cheerfully. On top of the cake was a tiny ballerina doll for decoration.

Mrs. Melrose went inside again, and Sumiko stood on the porch with the cake. She looked at the ballerina, listened to the music, looked at the door. She played the last few minutes over in her head. Uncle had left her not five minutes ago. She noticed a boy from her class peering at her from the window. Her face felt as hot as when she was lighting the fire under the tub. Then she felt furious! Without thinking, she knocked on the door. The maid opened up and waited, but at first Sumiko wasn't sure what she wanted to say. Then she blurted, "I need my present back." She wasn't going to let Uncle's money be wasted. That would be like they were stealing from him.

The maid retrieved the present and handed it coolly to Sumiko before shutting the door. Sumiko saw several of the other kids now watching her from a window. She took her cake and present down the steps and started to walk away. As Sumiko walked, her only thought was to get away. The problem was that she couldn't walk too far because Uncle and Jiichan were going to pick her up later.

She walked to Lane Street, where there were some small businesses. There was a bench near one store, so she sat on that and watched the clock on top of the bank across the street. She stared at the clock and felt disbelief that she wasn't at the party listening to Glenn Miller, but instead was sitting on a bench by herself. Like anyone, Sumiko had known momentary embarrassing moments, but right now she felt so overwhelmingly humiliated that it was as if nothing in her life would ever be the same again, as if everything she ever did—disbudding flowers, heating the water, cooking rice—would be different from now on. In the future she wouldn't be Sumiko who was disbudding flowers, she would be Humiliated Sumiko disbudding flowers. She wouldn't be Sumiko heating water and cooking rice, she would be Humiliated Sumiko heating water and cooking rice. And right at this moment she wasn't just Sumiko sitting alone on this bench, she was Humiliated Sumiko.

This is what it felt like to be lonely:

1. Like everyone was looking at you. Sumiko noticed that a few passersby were in fact looking at her sitting in her party dress, with her pretty pink gift on her lap and a piece of cake by her side.
2. Like nobody was looking at you. Sometimes the passersby didn't even glance at her.
3. Like you didn't care about anything at all. This happened for about thirty minutes. She felt a big blank inside of her.
4. Like you were just about to cry. This happened for the whole rest of the time she sat on the bench.

After a while she opened the present and took out the scarf. She left the wrapping on the bench and headed back toward the corner where Uncle was supposed to pick her up. Before she reached the corner, she balanced the cake in one hand and, with the other hand, stuffed the scarf into her underpants. She didn't even care if anyone saw her. Then she waited at the corner with her cake.

Uncle arrived early—she made it back just ahead of him. Jiichan sat in the passenger seat but scooted over for her. She climbed in and sat next to Jiichan. He and Uncle both beamed at her. Jiichan looked at the cake.

"Ohhhhh," he said. "Expensive. That cake expensive."

Uncle said, "We'll make a dessert out of that tonight! I'll put the ballerina in a glass case for you!"

They both looked so excited for her and so expectant that Sumiko felt obligated to say something cheerful. She exclaimed, "That was a fun party!" She couldn't bear to tell them the truth. They'd be too disappointed. Jiichan might even do something crazy like knock on the Melroses' door and scold them. Or try to beat up Mr. Melrose and two of his friends!

Uncle said, "Did they ask you to sing?"

"Yes, I sang for three minutes, and everybody applauded."

Jiichan's face grew so proud and he smiled so hard, Sumiko thought his teeth were about to pop out.

Uncle said, "Your aunt told me to ask you if they have a nice house."

She hesitated before saying harshly, "It wasn't as nice as I was expecting." Uncle looked disappointed, so Sumiko said, "But it was very nice. The couch was velvet. The doorways were arched." He shook his head in admiration of the velvet couch and arched doorways.

"Did the kitchen have nice tiles?" her uncle asked.

Tiles?

"You know how your aunt has always wanted a kitchen with pretty tiles," Uncle added.

"Yes, they were pretty."

"With a hand-painted design?" Uncle asked.

She pretended to think. "I guess so."

"That's what I would have thought."

After a couple of minutes of driving, Jiichan and Uncle both commented on how quiet she was and Jiichan worried that she might have caught something at the party.

She forced herself to chatter as much as she could, but it was tiring. Dinner was even more tiring. Everybody asked her questions and then oohed and aahed when she answered. At some point, for no reason, Jiichan exclaimed, "Maybe someday you be prom queen!"

A couple of times Auntie said she looked pale and felt her forehead. Everybody ate a thin slice of the cake for dessert. The cake was proclaimed delicious. Finally, thankfully, dinner ended. After she cleared the table, Sumiko stood for a few minutes in front of the photograph that sat on the bureau behind the dining-room table. In the photograph Jiichan and her mother, father, aunt, and uncle stood solemnly in front of a curtain. The ladies wore kimonos, the men suits. Some of Jiichan's hair was black, and he held a small Japanese flag. Whenever she examined the picture, she could feel everybody in the house staring at her back. She imagined they were feeling sorry for her because she didn't have parents.

She went into the kitchen and began filling the sink with water, but Auntie called out, "You don't have to wash dishes tonight!" The little ballerina lay on the counter next to the sink. Sumiko dropped it to the floor and mashed it under her slipper. Then she threw it out the window.

Sumiko went to bed early and listened to the crickets sing while the rest of the family played cards in the living room. Once, to make herself feel better, she reached under her mattress to look at the receipt book she'd found on the street a year ago. She sometimes filled out the receipts and pretended she was selling flowers at her own shop. She loved her receipt book.

When Tak-Tak came in for bed later, she didn't say a word. Eventually, the house grew still.

And so Sumiko could finally allow herself to think about that minute alone on the porch, with the other children staring at her from the window. And she could finally allow herself to cry. She had wanted so badly to go to that party. She had wanted so badly to look pretty in her dress. She had wanted so, so badly to make friends with some of those girls.

She didn't even notice the door open, but suddenly Bull was by the bed, one of his big mittlike hands wiping her wet face. She sat up and sobbed in his arms. He was so big and wide, she couldn't reach her arms around him. In the dim light she saw Tak-Tak step around the curtain of blankets. She cried out to him, "Leave me alone!"

"What did I do?" he said.

Bull turned and said quietly, "Go to bed, Takao. I'll be right there to say good night." He spoke kind of in grunts, the way a bull would speak if bulls could speak. She sobbed so hard, she couldn't get her breath. Bull handed her a handkerchief. When she blew her nose, it felt like her brain was coming out of her nostrils.

"I can fix it, you know," he said.

"What?"

"The ballerina. My mother found it on the porch."

She cried even harder but remembered to lower her voice so Tak-Tak wouldn't hear. "Bull, they wouldn't let me come in the house! I didn't go to the party! They made me leave!" She tried to cry silently, but it just made her snort when she inhaled. She lowered her voice even more. "But, Bull, is it just because we're Japanese?"

Bull didn't answer for so long that Sumiko thought he hadn't heard her. But then he grunted, "Yes."

"Only that?"

"Yes." Then he said, *"Gaman."* That meant "We must bear it."

After a while Bull pushed her away, and she could see he was smiling gently. "Look at that," he said. He was gazing outside.

She followed his gaze and saw Uncle standing in the moonlight near the outhouse, talking to it and occasionally gesturing with his arms. Whenever Sumiko saw someone talking to the outhouse, she always knew exactly where Jiichan was. She and Bull laughed, and at last she was sleepy.

5

SUMIKO DIDN'T WAKE UP EARLY THE NEXT MORNING, and nobody woke her up. She wondered whether that meant they all knew about the party now. She dressed and then slapped and rubbed her face to try to bring blood to her skin.

She pulled the silk scarf from under the mattress, where she'd put it the day before. The scarf made her feel humiliated all over again, so she stuffed it back under her mattress. After that she went into the living room.

Jiichan was sitting in his chair reading the newspaper. He glanced at her.

"You go one party and now you think you can

wake up late?" He scowled. That meant Bull hadn't told anyone, and neither had Tak-Tak.

"Good morning, Jiichan."

"You look sick," he said. "Eyes puffy."

"I'm fine."

"You look sick. Go tell your auntie you're sick."

Sumiko wished she *were* sick. She certainly didn't feel like working today. Sunday was her day for housecleaning and reading Japanese. If she had questions about the Japanese, she would ask Jiichan.

"Where's Tak-Tak?" she asked.

"Outside with horse. He get bored waiting for sleepyhead."

Jiichan read his Japanese newspaper the whole morning. Every so often he would say things to Sumiko like, "Get me tea" or "You start rice yet?" or "Rub my feet." Taking care of old men's feet was one of a woman's jobs, according to Auntie. Auntie used to rub Jiichan's feet until one day he accused her of trying to break his big toe. Now it was Sumiko's job.

She was rubbing his toes when she heard honking from the road. She went to the front window and saw a car that looked like Mr. Hirata's driving alongside Mrs. Takahashi as she ran down the road crying. Mrs. Takahashi didn't pay any attention to the car. Where could she be going? She lived in the opposite direction. She was seventy-three years old. Sumiko had rarely seen her walk, let alone run. The car pulled up in front of Sumiko's house. It *was* Mr. Hirata—the sweet pea king. Mrs. Takahashi kept crying and ran right past the house. Sumiko opened the door before Mr. Hirata could knock.

He was wearing his farm clothes, and his face was dirty. He breathed hard, even though he'd been driving. He removed his hat and bowed slightly to her.

"Sumi-chan. Is your uncle home?"

"He's out in the field." She paused. "Do you want to sit down?"

"No. May I talk to him?" Mr. Hirata asked, barely concealing his impatience.

Jiichan stood up, obviously insulted. "Can I help?"

Mr. Hirata bowed his head respectfully and said, "Matsuda-san, it's only that—I should talk to your son, too." He walked a couple of steps backward, nodding respectfully at Jiichan. Then he turned around and rushed through the living room with Sumiko following. They ran right through the kitchen and to the back door before he turned to her and said, "Stay here. This isn't for children."

The temperature was in the seventies, a perfect Southern California December day. The holes in parts of the old cheesecloth allowed the bright sun to shine on the carnations. Some days the brightness made the flowers look artificial, as if they were made of paper. But today Sumiko thought the flowers almost seemed to glow. At Mr. Ono's farm a man was running across a field. Maybe somebody had been hurt on a tractor. That's what was wrong the last time Sumiko had seen this much commotion.

When Mr. Hirata reached her uncle, everyone except Bull stopped working to watch. Auntie and Ichiro walked over. Tak-Tak was nowhere to be seen. Mr. Hirata was speaking loudly, but Sumiko couldn't make out what he was saying. Everybody started running across the field toward the house. Tak-Tak stepped out of the stable. Uncle called out sharply to him.

"Takao, get inside the house!"

Sumiko wondered who had been hurt and how badly. Then she had a terrible thought. Maybe a fishing boat on Terminal Island had sunk and more than one person had been hurt!

When the grown-ups had almost reached her, Sumiko started to call out a question, but Uncle snapped, "Get inside!" He half pushed her through the doorway. He was usually very mild mannered. Fear washed over Sumiko. Maybe a relative had been hurt in the fishing accident? Auntie had a cousin who fished off Terminal Island.

"What is it, Uncle?"

She followed them into the living room, where Uncle and Auntie gave each other one of their meaningful looks that nobody else ever knew the meaning of. They had been married since they were both twenty-one. Sumiko had the feeling that each knew exactly what the other was thinking. Their faces were pale.

Jiichan stood up, but then he sat down and said, "Nobody tell old man, that's okay, I don't care!" He pretended to be reading his newspaper. Still nobody spoke. Another long look passed between Uncle and Auntie. Jiichan said again, "I said I don't care!"

Uncle knelt on the floor and took Jiichan's hand as if Jiichan were a little child. "Hirata-san heard on the radio that Japan bombed Hawaii," Uncle said to Jiichan.

Jiichan looked stricken. He softly said something that sounded like "Wah." But Sumiko knew what he'd said: "War."

There was another long silence as Auntie and Uncle stared at each other. The way they looked at each other scared Sumiko. "Are they going to kill us?" she half whispered.

Auntie said, "Of course not. Don't talk like Tak-Tak."

Mr. Hirata cleared his throat, then bowed to the room and said to Uncle, "Good luck. Let's talk later."

He literally ran out the front door.

And again there was silence. Then Auntie announced, "We'll have to burn our things." She turned to Sumiko. "Get your notebooks that you practice Japanese in." To Tak-Tak she said, "Find all our Japanese books and magazines."

Tak-Tak rushed off.

Sumiko turned to run off, but then she turned right back to Auntie. "Burn our things?" she said. "What do you mean?" What did burning their things have to do with the Japanese bombing Hawaii?

"Anything that might make them suspicious."

"But why?" Sumiko said. "Suspicious of what?"

"Isoginasai!" Hurry!

Auntie looked so furious that Sumiko immediately ran out of the room to fetch her notebooks. She stopped in the hallway and turned back to the living room. "Auntie!" But Auntie wasn't listening. She was peering out the front window, so mesmerized that she didn't even notice Sumiko slip beside her. Sumiko saw a single tail of smoke rising in the distance.

"Others have already started," Auntie said fretfully.

No one answered her, but suddenly everyone except Bull was talking at once. Then everyone stopped and Bull spoke: "I should tend the flowers. We may need money." Uncle nodded, and Bull went out to the fields.

"I'm not going to burn my notebooks," Sumiko announced. She had worked hard to learn to write a little Japanese.

Uncle leaned over Sumiko and shook her shoulders just once, as if shaking sense into her. "If we are all arrested, who will take care of you? Now get your notebooks and anything else that seems un-American." He spoke so solemnly that Sumiko felt terrified. He spoke as if he himself might be arrested simply because she could write Japanese. She ran to her closet.

For a long while she just stood in her closet holding her notebooks close to her. Jiichan had paid old Mrs. Ige to help her write better. Mrs. Ige had also taught Sumiko's mother.

By the time Sumiko got outside, Uncle had already started the fire on the dirt ground between the house and the flower fields. The wood in the fire looked like it had come from the bathhouse. Sumiko saw that on the Ono farm the Onos also had started a fire. Sumiko held her notebooks tightly.

Then she saw it.

"That's the picture from the bureau!" she cried. "You can't get arrested for that! That's my parents!" She grabbed the stick her uncle was using to stoke the fire, but he took a firm hold of her arm.

"There's a Japanese flag in that picture," said Uncle. "It's dangerous to keep it."

She turned to her grandfather. "Jiichan!"

But for once Jiichan had nothing to say. He just scowled at her as if she were misbehaving.

Sumiko held her notebooks up and whispered, "Bye." Then she flung them into the fire and watched them smoke and turn black. It looked like a disease had struck the papers. The fire heated Sumiko's face. Ashes flew around her like insects. She suddenly remembered something she'd never remembered before: ashes flying around a fire as she and her parents burned garbage in an incinerator; her mother saying, "Wish on the floating ash, Sumi-chan"; and Sumiko wishing. But she couldn't remember what she'd wished.

Now she didn't move until every page had turned black and shriveled. Then Auntie made her run inside to find more things to burn. She didn't know what might be considered "disloyal." If notebooks were somehow disloyal, then was a Japanese silk fan also bad? And what about her kimono? Surely there was nothing dangerous about a kimono. She picked hers up, but then decided to push it far back into her closet.

Except for Bull, the family spent the rest of the day combing the house for anything that seemed Japanese in a disloyal way, whatever that meant.

By bedtime Sumiko was exhausted. In the surrounding fields a multitude of fires lit up the black night. She felt she could no longer stand up. Tak-Tak was already asleep when she got to the bedroom. His face was black with ash. She wiped his face, but he didn't even notice. She wiped listlessly at her own face. She remembered that she hadn't heated the water tonight, just as she hadn't yesterday. But nobody had said anything about it either time. She sat up in her bed and saw that, outside, her aunt and uncle were standing in the glare of the fire. Whereas earlier they had seemed feverish, now they seemed automated and emotionless. Bull was probably in the stable, talking to Baba. Bull had continued to work even after dark. She knew he would make sure they didn't run out of money.

Later, long after she had gotten in bed, Sumiko could hear adult voices from the living room. Finally she sneaked into the hallway to listen.

"A friend of mine got beat up last week," Ichiro was saying. "Some *hakujin* did it." *Hakujin* were white people.

Then there was silence until Bull said, "Dad, is the rifle still in the closet?"

"No, I already took it down. It's under my bed," Sumiko heard her uncle say.

Sumiko felt a chill at the word "rifle." She'd seen the rifle only once, a couple of years ago, when there was a burglar active in the community. The burglar was never caught, and Sumiko never saw the rifle again. She turned around and found Tak-Tak standing beside her. His mouth was hanging open. He looked terrified.

The grown-ups started getting ready for bed, and Sumiko led Tak-Tak back to their room. "I'll keep the blankets open," she whispered to him as he crawled in bed. She pulled the blankets apart.

"Okay?" she said.

"Okay," he said.

In the distance Mr. Ono had not turned on the lights over his fields. His fire was still going strong. It was as if he no longer cared if his chrysanthemums bloomed early or not. All he cared about was burning his things.

6

THE NEXT DAY THE UNITED STATES DECLARED WAR ON Japan. The declaration was a different kind of shock from the Pearl Harbor attack. Pearl Harbor was like a big noise, and the declaration of war was like a big silence. Sumiko stayed home from school. Since Auntie or Uncle didn't tell her why she had to stay home from school, she decided it was so that nobody would take her POW or hostage. Also, on the radio she'd heard a governor from another state announce that if any "Japs" living in California tried to come to his state, they would soon be hanging from trees.

Sumiko kept checking out the front window to see if anybody was coming to get them. But all day the road was quiet. Bull continued to work the fields, while Uncle, Jiichan, Ichiro, and even Auntie went to meetings with other people in the community.

In the early afternoon Auntie rushed into the house with her face flushed from fear and excitement. Sumiko had been scrubbing the rice pot but set it down and ran to Auntie. Auntie collapsed on the floor and held on to the side of a kitchen chair.

"Auntie!" Sumiko put her arms around her, something she had never done before. She loved Auntie, and Auntie loved her, but Auntie did not like hugs. Auntie liked worrying and working and scolding.

There was a knock at the door, and Auntie suddenly shot to her feet and exclaimed, "Oh!" She took a pouch from her coat pocket and handed it to Sumiko, hissing, "Hide this."

Sumiko didn't wait to hear more, just ran crazily to her bedroom and stuffed the pouch under the mattress. Her pounding heart quieted when she heard Mr. Hirata speaking in Japanese to Auntie. They were talking about somebody getting arrested. Sumiko couldn't stop herself from lifting the mattress and opening the pouch. All it held was one twenty-dollar bill. She pushed it under the mattress again and hurried to the living room just as Jiichan and Uncle rushed in. Nobody paid any attention to her.

Mr. Hirata looked at Jiichan. "The FBI came for my father. They started arresting the community leaders and the *Issei* yesterday. It's still going on today." *Issei* meant the first generation—those born in Japan who immigrated to the United States for a better life. "I heard they took the principal of the Japanese school. And they took Isoda-san because he was the principal of a Japanese school in Washington fifteen years ago. They searched his house and found many books written in Japanese."

Jiichan had once been principal of the Japanese school. Sumiko said, "We have to hide Jiichan!"

Jiichan knelt, and hugged Sumiko quietly for a moment. Then he said, "I better pack."

Sumiko said, "Good, you can hide at Mr. Ono's house."

He turned to walk out, moving as if he were very old. He *was* old, but he'd never walked that way before. She started to chase after him, but he turned and held up his palm in the *stop* gesture.

Auntie told Sumiko to clean up the house. Sumiko cried out, "But what about Jiichan? Mr. Ono will let him hide at his house!" Cleaning was ridiculous at a time like this.

Auntie pushed Sumiko toward the kitchen. "I said clean up."

"But everything's clean."

"Then clean it again!"

So Sumiko scrubbed the entire house. All that afternoon, whenever she passed through the living room, she saw Jiichan sitting in his special chair with his old suitcase on the floor beside him. That suitcase was so old, Sumiko thought it might have come on the ship to America with him decades earlier.

"Jiichan?" she said.

"Hmm."

"Do you want me to rub your foot?"

"Just one? You make me unbalanced." He didn't smile, so she wasn't sure if he was kidding.

"I can rub both." For an answer, he kicked off his slippers. She rubbed his left foot for a while, then rubbed his right foot in exactly the same way so she wouldn't make him unbalanced. She rubbed his feet in all the magic places that gave him peace.

After that she did her farm chores and cooked a new pot of rice. When she heard a firm knock at the door, she knew it was someone to take her grandfather. She ran into the living room. Everyone was there except Bull, who was probably still working. But nobody answered the door. The knock came harder, and Tak-Tak shouted out, "Get the rifle!" Auntie slapped him, then gaped at her own hand as if it weren't attached to her. Tak-Tak stared at her. Sumiko pulled him into her chest and pressed her nose into his hair.

Auntie finally answered the door. Two white men in suits stood on the porch with two police officers.

None of the men took off their hats to speak to Auntie. One of them said, "We'd like to talk to Masanori Matsuda." That was Jiichan! He picked up his suitcase and walked to the door.

"I am Masanori Matsuda."

"We'd like to take you and your son to our office to ask you some questions."

"My son?" Jiichan appeared to lose his balance for a moment but quickly regained it.

Ichiro stepped forward and called out, "I'm an American. Can you tell me where you are taking them?"

One of the men turned to Ichiro. "Are you Hatsumi?"

Uncle stepped forward. "I am Hatsumi. May I pack?"

"We're running late."

And just like that, Jiichan with his suitcase and Uncle without his followed the men up the sidewalk. The rest of the family trailed along. Sumiko saw Mr. Ono already sitting in the backseat of the car.

"Mr. Ono!" Sumiko cried out.

As if deeply ashamed, Mr. Ono hung his head and didn't meet Sumiko's eyes.

The car drove off. "You shamed Ono-san," Auntie scolded her.

Sumiko knew one of the things that made her different from the rest of her family, one of the things that made her more American than her cousins, was that she didn't feel *haji*, or shame, quite as much as other Japanese did, maybe because she hadn't attended a lot of Japanese school. All the *Issei* were steeped in the culture of *haji*. Years ago Mr. Ono had been mistakenly arrested—the police then were actually searching for a different Mr. Ono. But today Mr. Ono still felt *haji* over his mistaken arrest.

The family just sat in the living room. They didn't even eat dinner. Sumiko couldn't remember ever having not eaten dinner. At one point Ichiro went and got the rifle, and then they all sat silently with the rifle leaning on the couch. At another point Sumiko cried out, "Aren't we going to do anything?" but Auntie just shot her an angry look.

Every now and then Bull looked outside at the dark fields, no doubt concerned about what would happen to the flowers.

Nobody even bothered to turn on a light as they sat in the living room throughout the evening.

Then a terrible thought occurred to Sumiko. "Will Uncle and Jiichan be tortured?"

"I don't know," Ichiro said.

That night Auntie went to her room early and wailed so loudly, Sumiko could hear her even though her bedroom was across the house.

When Sumiko herself went to bed and pulled the blanket room divider shut, she examined the items under her mattress: Auntie's pouch; Sumiko's own savings of six dollars from occasionally helping on the other farms; the receipt book; and the silk scarf that had cost Uncle four dollars. She felt sick with guilt about the cost of the scarf.

She heard the crickets, and she saw that someone had turned Mr. Ono's lights on over the chrysanthemums.

Tak-Tak said, "Sumiko?"

"Yes?"

"Uncle taught me how to use the rifle. I can protect you."

"Don't talk like that!" But she could feel in the darkness that he was about to cry now, so she added, "Thank you, I know you'll protect me."

And she knew he would.

7

WHEN SUMIKO OPENED HER EYES THE NEXT MORNING, her first thought was, This is day three. Auntie came in as the room was just getting light. She held her finger to her mouth to shush Sumiko.

"Where's my pouch?" she whispered.

"It's under the bed," Sumiko whispered back.

"Did you look inside?"

"Yes," Sumiko admitted.

"That's all right. We'll leave the money there for now. They've frozen all the accounts at our bank. I managed to get that much out, but I wasn't able to get to our main bank in time. Why don't you children sleep in today? I don't want you going to school until things have settled down."

Auntie left, and Sumiko heard her brother's bed squeak. She got up and peered around the blankets.

"Auntie says to sleep in today."

He lay still for a moment. Sumiko got back in bed.

After a time Tak-Tak said, "But I'm not sleepy."

"Just concentrate on falling back to sleep," Sumiko said. "Find the sleep in your head."

Tak-Tak said, "I can't. Aren't you going to school?"

"No," Sumiko said.

"But you have a math test."

Sumiko lay with her eyes wide open and counted to five hundred. "Well, that's enough, I'm getting up," she said.

She didn't look over her dresses in the closet, just walked straight to the bureau to grab slacks and an old blouse. Tak-Tak squinted at her.

"I can't find my glasses."

Sumiko went to his bed to look around. His glasses lay on the floor with the lenses facedown. He stuck them on. The elastic band pushed his hair straight up. She smiled.

"Why are you smiling?"

"Because you look like a pineapple." He seemed to think that over as she matted down his hair.

After they were dressed, they went into the kitchen. For the second day in a row nobody went to the flower market. Sumiko walked through the fields and saw valuable flowers turning past their prime. She'd never seen their flowers go to waste before. It was almost like watching an animal die and not trying to help.

Their whole lives revolved around getting the flowers to market. For a special treat Uncle had occasionally taken her and Tak-Tak to the market. They went to bed early and got up at midnight and rode in the truck to Los Angeles with him. They got to eat waffles and chow mein at the café next to the market. Everybody in the market was Japanese; across the street was the so-called American market. That was where the *hakujin* flower sellers worked.

Sumiko wondered if the Japanese market was empty today. She looked all around her. The fields seemed funny without Uncle and Jiichan out there. Thinking about them made Sumiko's stomach hurt. She wished she knew where they were. She was glad Jiichan had packed before he left.

Sumiko was back to work grading by midday. At midnight Ichiro planned to take the flowers to the market. He and Bull kept saying, "We might need money."

Sumiko felt like she was in limbo for the following weeks. All she did was work and wait for whatever might come next. Some *Nikkei* kids did return to school, but others, like Sumiko, were kept at home. On those rare occasions when Sumiko went to buy meat or vegetables with Auntie, the Christmas decorations she saw in store windows seemed out of place. Christmas was the last thing on her mind.

For Christmas, Auntie cooked a turkey, but the family had decided that to save money, nobody should give gifts. Christmas meant absolutely nothing to Sumiko that year.

On New Year's Day they usually attended a party at Mr. Muramoto's big house. His house was just as nice as Marsha Melrose's. But this year, for the first time in twenty years, Mr. Muramoto did not hold his annual New Year's Day party. Sumiko and what was left of her family went outside on New Year's evening to pray and meditate, something they'd never done together.

Bull, who had probably never given a speech in his life, said a few soft words about what he called the world of change. In the world of change you accept the changes that can't be helped. You suffer so you can learn, and you learn so you can be a better person in your next life. The cool night air blew on Sumiko's face while Bull spoke. She sniffed softly at the scent of flowers, much weaker at night than in the mornings, when the air was thick with fragrance. She had often tried to decide which was nicer, the mysterious night scent or the intense day scent.

Ichiro started talking about how angry he was over everything that was happening to them. Bull nodded his head. Sumiko knew he admired and respected Ichiro a great deal. But he didn't express anger himself.

When Ichiro stopped talking, Sumiko prayed for safety for her uncle and grandfather and Mr. Ono. She'd once heard their Buddhist minister say that it wasn't the Buddhist way to pray for something specific for yourself. But it's my way, Sumiko thought. And she repeated to herself in her head, Please keep them safe.

8

ICHIRO BROUGHT HOME NEWSPAPERS EVERY DAY. HE made Sumiko wait until he was finished with every word before she could touch the papers. She tried to read from the back, but if he caught her, he made her stop because he said it annoyed him. In the evenings the family listened to the radio together. It was strange to hear governors and other important people talking about her as if she were dangerous. One of the strangest things she heard was when one American general said of the *Nikkei*, "The very fact that no sabotage has taken place to date is a disturbing and confirming indication that such action will be taken."

Sumiko would sit at her window at night and think about the puzzle of those words: *The very fact that no sabotage has taken place to date is a disturbing and confirming indication that such action will be taken*. She'd memorized that line. As far as she could tell, what the general was saying was that since not a single instance of *Nikkei* sabotage had occurred, that confirmed such sabotage would take place in the future. So if the Japanese behaved themselves perfectly well and didn't break any laws, their *good* behavior could be taken as evidence of bad intentions. But she also knew that if they did break laws, their *bad* behavior would also be taken as evidence of bad intentions. Either way, they were doomed.

In February anyone of Japanese ancestry was restricted to a nighttime curfew until 6 AM. Ichiro broke curfew every day to travel to the flower market.

One night Sumiko got up to talk to him before he left. He was eating the breakfast she'd prepared for him the night before.

"Ichiro?"

"Why aren't you in bed?" he said tiredly.

"I wanted to ask you something." She felt wide awake. "What if some soldiers stop you?"

"They stop me almost every day."

"They do? What do they say?"

"They ask me what I'm doing, and I show them the flowers in the truck, and they let me go. Get to bed now. Don't you have to work on the carnations tomorrow?"

"Yes," she said.

"Get your rest, then."

Back in bed she thought about how much she liked the flower mart. Someday when she owned her shop, she would go to the market to pick out the best flowers. She imagined being on the outside of the market instead of on the inside. The most exciting moments of the morning at the market were when the opening bell rang, the accordion gate opened, and the customers rushed in like a wave. She liked to imagine riding that wave right into the flowers.

By the end of February more than two thousand *Nikkei* had been arrested without being charged with a crime. Many elders, as well as anyone who was a leader in the community, had been arrested. Uncle had once been president of a *Nikkei* flower growers association, plus he was born in Japan. Ichiro had heard that the FBI had been keeping files on *Nikkei* leaders for years.

Auntie got a letter from Uncle saying that he and Jiichan were in a prison camp in North Dakota. He warned Auntie to cooperate with authorities. Some of his letter was blacked out by censors. Sumiko took the letter outside and held it up to the sun to see if she could read beneath the black marks, but she couldn't read a thing. Maybe the blacked-out parts were about the weather. Jiichan hated the cold. She worried he'd get sick.

Then suddenly *Nikkei* residents of the fishing community on Terminal Island were told by the government that they had forty-eight hours to evacuate the island, bringing only what they could carry. Many fishermen had been arrested as potential spies, and the wives who remained spoke little English. Some Japanese, even those without much money, owned beautiful wood furniture. From her cousin, Auntie heard stories about swarms of people who had descended on the island and bought up all the beautiful furniture for a fraction of its worth.

Every new law and development sent the community into an uproar. But the weird thing was that throughout all the furor, Sumiko's daily life hardly changed. She disbudded flowers, she graded and bunched them, she heated the bathwater. And she never went to school.

In March people of Japanese ancestry were given one week to evacuate Bainbridge Island near Seattle. Unlike the evacuees from Terminal Island, those from Bainbridge Island were to be taken to "reception centers." Ichiro said "reception centers" meant "big jails." The evacuees could bring only what they could carry and needed to dispose of all their personal effects beforehand. As at Terminal Island, people swarmed over the neighborhood to buy up household goods—and property—for a cheap price.

Sumiko went outside many nights and knelt among her peach *kusabana*. She filled her lungs with the smell of cloves and dirt. Amid all that was going on, she managed to feel calm out there among her flowers.

A few weeks later Ichiro called a family meeting after dinner. They sat in the living room waiting for him to speak. Finally he said, "I've decided we need to think about abandoning the farm and getting out of California."

Auntie laid her palm on her chest. "The Miyamotos tried to leave for Nevada. Some men with rifles met them and turned them back."

"How would we make a living in another state?" Bull said. "Should we just leave behind the flowers?"

Nobody asked Sumiko's opinion, but she gave it anyway. "I want to stay on my farm," she said.

"Where would we go?" Bull said doubtfully. "And what if they decide not to evacuate us after all?"

"The governor of Colorado spoke out in defense of us. I thought we could go there."

Bull frowned. "Here we can support ourselves. And—" He frowned even more deeply. "And the flowers. How can we leave them?"

"We can't leave the flowers!" Sumiko said. "Who'll take care of them?"

"What does it matter?" Ichiro said.

"But it does matter!" She tried to think why. "It matters because the flowers are—they're—everything we do depends on the flowers!"

Auntie said, "We should stay here where we're with other Japanese."

Ichiro said, "All of you think about it, and we'll have another meeting tomorrow."

But the meeting never happened, for the next day the decision was made for them when the government announced that *Nikkei* were prohibited from voluntary evacuation of the West Coast. They were, basically, under arrest. They could not leave the area.

9

One morning Sumiko noticed that they'd all begun to look at their belongings differently, assessing what items might be worth good money. They started eating at the kitchen table for dinner to avoid getting the dining-room table dirty, just in case they needed to sell it.

More areas had been evacuated. But a couple of reliable men in the neighborhood had heard that Sumiko's community wouldn't be evacuated until June. So Sumiko's family was pretty surprised in May when a sign appeared in a neighborhood not far from where they lived. The sign announced that in one week all *Nikkei* in the area would be evacuated to a temporary center at a racetrack. Sumiko was filled with a weird feeling then, a feeling she never would have expected: relief. Finally the moment they'd feared was here!

Bull and Ichiro went out the next day, as required, to register the family with the government and receive a family ID number.

Suddenly hundreds of people in the area were selling cars, furniture, and tractors. Auntie moaned at her stupidity for not selling their furniture earlier. Whenever Sumiko looked out the front window, she saw *hakujin* driving down the dirt road. Sometimes the cars stopped at Sumiko's house. Their house had become a store. People by the dozens tramped through, touching their things and offering them much less than the items were worth.

Every day men looked at Baba but declined to buy her. Sumiko and Tak-Tak would spend an hour each evening sitting on the stable floor with the horse. Sometimes Tak-Tak would brush Baba down, but other times he would just sit on the ground and sing songs with Sumiko, to keep Baba company during these last days with her as their horse. Tak-Tak even begged to sleep in the stable, but Auntie said no.

One day Sumiko and Tak-Tak were in their room playing cards when Bull entered. He set Tak-Tak in his lap and said, "Someday I'll get you all the horses you want."

Tak-Tak's eyes lit up. "I want twenty—twenty-one counting Baba!"

"Okay, I'll get you twenty." Bull seemed exhausted. Nobody spoke for a moment, and Bull continued quietly. "I've sold Baba. At least she'll have a home now."

Tak-Tak's mouth fell open, and he made a little choking noise. His face got all screwed up, but at first he didn't cry at all. He ran outside, Sumiko following.

When they reached the stable, it was, of course, empty. Then Tak-Tak cried and cried. Sumiko sat with him in the hay for an hour, until his sobs turned to whimpers. They went inside and found their beds had been sold.

That night they lay on the floor where their beds used to be. Auntie wanted them to keep sleeping in their room because she had the crazy idea that this would help "keep things normal." But no curtains hung in the window, and moonlight slashed shadows across the barren room. Tak-Tak seemed all cried out.

Bull came in to say good night. First he went to Tak-Tak and said that he had decided to make him a special box to carry his crickets in when they evacuated. "Thank you," Tak-Tak said glumly.

When Bull said good night to Sumiko, he asked, "Is there anything you need?"

"No. Bull, I'm sorry about Baba."

"It's over now," he said.

"What was the man like who bought her?"

Bull didn't answer, and Sumiko knew that the rest of Baba's life would not be pleasant. Finally Bull said resignedly, "How much did you sell that scarf for?"

"A dollar."

"Almost as much as for the horse," he said.

"There are more horses for sale than expensive silk scarves."

"All right," he said, instead of "good night." The shadows cut his back in two as he walked out. Sumiko lifted her blankets and went over to Tak-Tak. She lay down and put her arms around him.

He felt strange and cold, not like a living boy. "When do you think you'll have your flower shop?" he said.

"Maybe when I'm twenty-five."

"Do you think Baba will still be alive?"

"I don't think so," she said. She pressed her nose into his hair. He pulled away.

"Do you think Ichiro will make a lot of money?"

"He says he will."

"When?" he said.

"I don't know."

"Before you own your flower shop?"

She thought that over, then said, "Yes, he'll be successful first because he's older."

"Do you think he can buy Baba back?"

She started to say she didn't think so, but instead she said, "Yes."

"Are you sure?"

"Yes," she lied. "I'm sure."

10

On the day they left their house forever, Sumiko put on her mint green school dress.

She went outside to see everything for the last time. She wanted to sit amid the *kusabana* but didn't want to dirty her dress. Instead, she just stood in the middle of the fields and gazed out at the weedflowers, at the orderly rows of carnations, and at the ranunculus plants that would bloom through the summer if someone filled the irrigation ditches. The *kusabana* already seemed a little unruly, and the bathhouse already seemed foreign. The shed just made her sad. Then she thought for the first time in a while of Uncle's special room.

Sumiko went into the shed and pushed open the door of Uncle's room. She felt guilty, since she'd never been allowed in there. The room was tidy and plain, with a few dead carnations in containers. On the shelves sat several envelopes labeled in Uncle's neat writing and probably filled with seeds. Sumiko picked up the envelopes and smiled weakly. Uncle had named his new strains after members of the family. She looked inside one labeled STOCK—SUMIKO STRAIN.

Auntie was calling for her. Sumiko took the SUMIKO STRAIN envelope outside with her.

Auntie stood in the middle of the yard. "What have you been doing?"

"Getting flower seeds."

"Have you finished packing?" Auntie's forehead was a mass of wrinkles.

"Almost." Sumiko rushed back inside, where she tucked the seeds into her suitcase.

The families were supposed to bring their own linens, and that took up a lot of space. Besides the seeds, Sumiko brought her yellow knife, because it was just about the only special possession she had left. She also carried some extra clothes for her brother. She worried because Tak-Tak couldn't carry much. But then she heard Bull saying, "Sumiko can't carry much."

Nobody in the neighborhood knew where they'd all end up after the temporary center, but nearly everybody assumed it would be somewhere cold, like where Uncle and Jiichan and the other arrested men had been confined after they were "processed." Sumiko hoped her entire family would be sent to the same place. Anyway, she had packed all their warmest clothes: boots and heavy sweaters and heavy slacks. Sumiko also had packed two school dresses for herself and two nice outfits for Tak-Tak.

Before they left, Bull brought in a box poked through with pinholes. "For the crickets," he said. "The cage is too bulky." He'd attached a string to the box so that Tak-Tak could hang it over his shoulder.

The man who was buying their truck had agreed to take them to the street where all the *Nikkei* from the area were supposed to await government transportation to the racetrack. The truck's buyer was a quiet man who seemed a little embarrassed by how little he had paid for the vehicle. He didn't meet anyone's gaze full on.

Sumiko, Tak-Tak, and Bull sat in back with the luggage. She stared at the farm as they drove off. The flower fields rippled like a flag. Probably someone else would be moving in soon. Ichiro said they would not be allowed to return to the coast before the war ended, if ever. If the war lasted for ten years, she would be twenty-two at the end. She might already be married and living with her husband's family.

Sumiko hoped someone would take over the farm quickly. Otherwise, all that work they'd done would be wasted.

As they drove, Sumiko saw that the community was deserted. Nobody worked the land, no kids played in the yards, no old people sat on their front porches. Cheesecloth shuddered over the lonely fields. In many houses, Sumiko saw signs hanging in the windows: I AM AN AMERICAN.

Leaving this way made Sumiko love what she'd always loved—the colors, the smells—but it made her also love what she thought she'd hated. For instance, she'd often hated the drafts in the bathhouse, but now she remembered how delicious and precious the last vestiges of warmth in the tub had seemed.

In the distance Sumiko spotted several abandoned dogs running through some flowers, smashing them. Humane societies in evacuation areas were supposedly overflowing. Mrs. Ono hadn't been able to find someone to adopt her dog, and she refused to have the animal put down. Instead, she had left several open bags of food in her house and tacked a note about the dog on her front door. Sumiko thought nobody would want a "Jap" dog.

Bull was looking at his hands now, his forehead crinkled between his eyebrows.

"Do you think we'll ever come back?" Sumiko said.

Bull looked up distractedly. "Probably not."

Sumiko stared at her old neighborhood until it disappeared from sight.

As they neared the drop-off point the street grew crowded with *Nikkei* families and their luggage. Sumiko felt panicked, wondering suddenly whether her family could just abandon their possessions and simply *run*. Run and run and run—but to where? The only religious group at a national level speaking up for the Japanese was the Quakers. Maybe her family could find some Quakers and hide out with them. She wondered whether any Quakers lived nearby.

She wondered how Baba was doing.

Sumiko had tied a tag with their family ID number to Tak-Tak's jacket button. She tightened the string. On the streets she saw other young children with tags on their buttons. The street was as silent as if it were deserted. All the girls wore their school dresses, and their faces looked scared and unhappy, which was exactly how Sumiko felt.

When the truck stopped, Bull said to Tak-Tak, "Hold on to Sumiko. Don't let go until we get to the assembly center. Do you hear me?"

Tak-Tak nodded.

Bull put on his hat and jumped off to help Ichiro unload the family's belongings. Bull owned just one hat; Ichiro used to own a dozen but had kept only the one on his head. It was his most expensive hat, but it looked out of place now.

On the sidewalk Tak-Tak clung to Sumiko, and she clung to him.

The man buying their truck reached out to shake Ichiro's hand. Ichiro hesitated so slightly that Sumiko did not think the man noticed. They shook hands.

"Look, there's Mrs. Ono," said Sumiko. "Mrs. Ono!" The old woman stood alone and crying. Sumiko ran over to take her arm while Ichiro and Bull carried her baggage.

As soon as Mrs. Ono reached Auntie, she blurted out, "I hope my dog doesn't eat all his food at once." She sobbed and leaned on Sumiko.

Everything was so sad. Sumiko couldn't think of one happy thing.

A big rumbling sound was growing louder. Sumiko saw a line of army trucks approaching, and she pulled Tak-Tak tightly to her. "Careful!" she said, though the trucks were still far away.

When the trucks parked, everybody on the sidewalks surged toward them. Bull and Ichiro helped other people load their things while Sumiko and Tak-Tak clung to each other on the sidewalk. Sumiko had been watching people climb up when she suddenly realized that she and Tak-Tak were two of the last Japanese standing on the sidewalk. She cried out, "Where is every—" and then felt herself lifted into the air and into the truck. Then Bull lifted Tak-Tak in and jumped in himself. The truck made a tremendous rumbling noise, as if they were in the center of a thundering cloud. A soldier closed a canvas flap, and darkness enveloped the back of the truck.

11

WHEN THE RUMBLING FINALLY STOPPED, NOBODY MOVED.

A soldier came around to pull the canvas aside. Everybody got off. A big sign read SAN CARLOS RACETRACK. A tall stone wall encircled the track. Sumiko looked up at a guard tower and saw a soldier pointing a rifle at her. She froze, but then he moved his rifle toward another truck. Sumiko realized she had driven by here before, on the way to a picnic.

When soldiers opened the gate, Sumiko didn't move. Finally Ichiro led the way, Tak-Tak's crickets slung over his back.

Inside the racetrack Sumiko saw row after row of barracks. She followed Ichiro to a table, where a

Nikkei man checked them in. "You're assigned to Section Seven, Stable Four," the man said, as if everything were perfectly normal, as if he were saying something as mundane as, *The weather is nice today*. The man continued casually, "You can drop off your things and then return to pick up your cots and fill your mattresses with straw. Mattress bags are in the corner there. Next!"

Ichiro and the rest of the family walked off, and Sumiko chased after them.

Stables lined the walls of the racetrack, while the barracks sat in the center. There was not a tree in sight. Open trenches stretched across the front of some of the barracks, with planks of wood forming a bridge into the front door. Sumiko smelled sewage.

Tak-Tak grabbed her hand and said hopefully, "Will we live with a horse?"

"No," she said, although she honestly didn't know. In fact, she thought anything was possible now. She was still herself and her family were still themselves, but every other thing was different.

A few families were filling bags with straw. A sign said FILL MATTRESSES HERE.

"No horse?" said Tak-Tak. "Are they going to kill us?"

He spoke as if *no horse* and *kill us* were somehow related. "No, they're giving us mattresses," Sumiko said logically.

"So?"

"So they wouldn't give us mattresses if they were going to kill us." She watched him to see whether he thought that sounded as ridiculous to him as it suddenly did to her—as if *mattresses* were somehow related to *not killing us*. But he seemed satisfied.

Section Seven, Stable Four was at the far end of the grounds. Stable Four was part of a line of old wooden stables with chipping white paint. Ichiro stepped gingerly inside. Sumiko followed and then the others. Nobody spoke. It looked like a two-horse stable. It stank of manure and chlorine. Mushrooms grew in a corner. One lightbulb hung from above. Sumiko squinted at the bulb: twenty-five watts. She turned to Ichiro. "How are we going to live here?"

"What do you mean 'how'? We don't have a choice."

All afternoon they filled bags with straw and dragged them to their stable. Sometimes it seemed there were hundreds of people converging on the straw like flies. Ichiro had already found out that there would be almost twenty thousand people living in the racetrack until permanent camps were ready for them.

Sumiko did the only thing she knew to do when she was scared or sad: work hard. Working hard made Sumiko feel better—not good, but better.

After all the mattresses were filled, Sumiko tried

lying on her straw bed. It felt uneven and prickly. She rearranged it and tried again, but it felt exactly the same. Tak-Tak was trying his out too.

"It feels pokey," he said.

"I'll put on an extra sheet for you," Sumiko said.

A gong rang, and Sumiko looked at Ichiro to see what they should do. He and Bull stepped outside. Sumiko and Tak-Tak followed and saw dozens of screaming kids tearing through the aisles shouting, "Dinner! Dinner!"

Dinner was served in a huge, long room called a "mess hall." Everybody got their food on trays and went to sit at picnic tables. The entrée was cod stew. The other kids ate as if starving, and then ran out.

Sumiko's stomach rumbled all evening, even after their lone dim lightbulb had been turned off and everybody else was asleep. Later she woke up with a desperate need to use the bathroom. When she sat up, Tak-Tak said softly, "Sumiko?"

"Yes?"

"I pooped in my pajamas."

"All right, come on."

She switched on the bulb to find new clothes for him.

"What is it?" Auntie said sleepily.

"Tak-Tak needs new pants," she said. She'd packed only one pair of pajamas for him. She decided she'd put him in his long johns. "Come on." She took his hand.

A few steps outside their stable a searchlight caught them in its glare. Sumiko hissed, "Stay still." Tak-Tak froze, whimpering very softly. Then she looked up and saw a soldier standing beside the searchlight. She looked down and saw another searchlight following an old man toddling down an aisle. The beam that had been on her moved and crossed the other beam, and then it began to follow somebody else. She pulled her brother to the latrine. Despite the hour, there was a line outside.

"Everybody's got diarrhea from dinner," an old woman told her.

Inside the latrine was a line of holes in a wooden platform. Several old women sat on some holes. Sumiko cleaned off her brother's behind and put him in his long johns. On the way back to the stable the searchlight followed them again, the beam accentuating Tak-Tak's skinny legs.

Tak-Tak fell right asleep. But instead of sleeping, Sumiko lay on her straw, smelling manure and listening to her family breathe and imagining the world outside: houses and grocery stores and playgrounds. Auntie already had thought of a phrase to describe that world: *out there*. Sumiko remembered something she'd overheard Jiichan say once, that sometimes when you were low, all you had left in life was your right to close the door on the world and sit in your room alone where nothing further could befall you.

He had said he'd felt that way when Sumiko's mother died. He had closed the door to his room and separated himself from everything that was out there.

Beams from the searchlight reached inside through the stable slats and moved in flashes across the far wall. The searchlights were part of out there. At least Sumiko's family was in here. At least they had a door, and at least it was closed.

12

THE NEXT MORNING SUMIKO JUMPED OUT OF BED TO peek out the front door and see if the camp looked just the way she thought it had yesterday. For some reason she didn't know what to expect this morning. When she stepped out, not a thing had changed. Stables lined the outer wall, and barracks filled the center of the camp. Japanese people walked here and there, some of them looking dazed.

So they really were here, in a town enclosed by stone walls, and almost everybody else was out there. It all reminded her of something, but she couldn't remember what. Then she remembered. The place was like the dioramas her class had made for geography once. The class had formed groups, and each group had made a diorama of life in a different country. That was a lot of fun, a good memory from school. Sumiko had helped make the Paraguay diorama. The teacher said all the kids did a great job. But now Sumiko thought that if you had enlarged all the dioramas, there would have been things missing, like curtains, pets, and gardens. *Details*. Those details were also missing from the assembly center.

The bell sounded for breakfast. Throngs of kids were already running toward the mess hall and shouting.

Breakfast was about two tablespoons of scrambled eggs and two pieces of bacon the size of postage stamps. All the kids ate ravenously and then ran like mad to another mess hall to get more. Sumiko grabbed Tak-Tak and ran with the other kids.

After breakfast they took a walk, Tak-Tak holding tightly to Sumiko's blouse. As they walked Sumiko saw that many people had left their doors open for ventilation. So many cots filled some of the rooms in the barracks that there was no place to walk. The walls didn't extend all the way up, and you could see the beams in the ceilings. In one barrack three giggling boys were climbing across the beams peering into other people's homes.

"That looks fun," Tak-Tak said hopefully.

"I don't think we're supposed to do that."

"Will they shoot us?"

"Stop saying that. It's bad luck."

Sumiko opened the door to a barrack with a sign reading RECREATION. Inside she saw an empty room with a few tables. Seeing the empty room filled her with fear of something Jiichan had once described to her. He had been sick, and he tended to ramble when he was sick. Sumiko had been sitting with him as he told her about the trip from Japan to America. "I don't see sky for many long time. I feel close to ultimate boredom. That mean close to lose mind. Inside myself, I feel like screaming. Outside myself, I calm." He said that the thing that kept everybody going was a single word: *America*. That word was the most important thing his family owned, the only thing of value they possessed.

Day after day Sumiko felt as if she were living on the edge of the ultimate boredom. Some days she stayed inside the stable, other days she wandered aimlessly. Once as she and Tak-Tak wandered she heard people rushing through the aisles hissing, "The soldiers are checking for illegal sewing scissors!" She saw a woman screaming as soldiers ransacked her barrack.

Sumiko thought of her yellow knife and felt almost faint with fear as she ran to Stable Four. She could hear Tak-Tak calling behind her, "Where are we going?"

Auntie watched uncomprehendingly as Sumiko

ransacked her own luggage, found the knife, and ran outside. She stopped just long enough to snap at Tak-Tak, "You stay here!"

She ran and ran, finally stopping at the other end of the racetrack where she found a patch of dirt. She was drenched in sweat from running. She dug a hole and rammed her knife inside before walking back, trying to appear calm. She promised herself never to mention the knife to anyone.

Sumiko's next big surprise came a few days later when she noticed Mrs. Ono sobbing while holding a letter.

"Mrs. Ono? Can I help?" Sumiko asked.

Mrs. Ono couldn't stop crying as she waved the note in the air. She held on to Sumiko and sobbed and laughed. Sumiko took the note and read it:

Dear Mrs. Ono,

I hope this letter reaches you and would appreciate your letting me know. I am the new resident of your house. I wished to let you know that I will be caring for your dog until your release. Please do not worry as he is in good hands during these difficult times.

Yours truly,
Mrs. Julia Donnell

Reading the letter was like seeing the sky. Sumiko thought about the woman all day. It gave her so much hope, it seemed like a miracle.

One day Sumiko sneaked back to where she'd buried her knife. She dug it up and scratched off her name before burying it again.

Otherwise, every day was the same. Oh, there were more room searches and there were electrical blackouts and the kids were going wild, but for Sumiko, whether their barrack was dark or light didn't change her life much. Whether their barrack was ransacked by soldiers didn't change her life at all. They had nothing to hide anymore.

Then one evening in late May, Ichiro ran inside and said, "My friend says the camp paper is going to announce tomorrow that the government will start moving us all to a permanent relocation center."

The next day camp was in bedlam, people standing in the aisles shouting and discussing and debating and crying. The paper announced that several hundred to a thousand people would be shipped out at a time. Sumiko's family was on the list of those leaving first.

The next day she came across some kids she didn't know climbing a ladder up a roof. She hesitated—ladders were probably forbidden. But then she couldn't resist, and she clambered up behind them. As she neared the top she saw the kids gaping at something.

She hurried up and saw what they saw. It was something amazing: normal life. Cars drove, people walked, trees swayed in the wind. A couple of the kids on the roof started crying. Sumiko just stared in amazement.

Later when she got back to the stable, her family was packing. They'd found out the next day they were being shipped to Poston, Arizona. The only thing anyone seemed to know about Poston was that it was very hot there. She thought about the coats and sweaters that had filled the meager space in their suitcases. Her uncle and grandfather didn't have clothes for cold weather, and Sumiko, Tak-Tak, Auntie, Bull, and Ichiro didn't have clothes for warm weather. So as before when she'd left the farm, she now found herself almost liking what she thought she had hated. Here the weather was mild; Poston would be hot. Here life was predictable; she didn't know what Poston would be like. Here she had started to feel safe; who knew what would happen to them in Poston?

Her family walked through the aisles carrying their things. The camp was like a maze, with only the sun to tell Sumiko which way they were going. The nearer they got to the entrance gate, the more people joined them. Ichiro and Bull walked ahead, carrying the bulk of the family's belongings.

Sumiko was so worried, she thought she would explode. "Ichiro?"

Ichiro stopped and turned to her.

"Is it better to go or to stay here?"

"I have no idea," he said tiredly, and began walking again.

As they walked more and more people joined them. About a thousand *Nikkei* waited with their possessions at the gate. Hundreds of others had gathered to watch them leave.

Sumiko walked through the gate and thought about her knife. Maybe a hundred years from that moment, someone would dig it up. But probably nobody would ever see it again.

13

SUMIKO FOUND HERSELF IN ANOTHER DARK, RUMBLING TRUCK.

1. They wanted us to leave California.
2. They wouldn't let us leave California.
3. They wanted us in the racetrack.
4. They don't want us in the racetrack.
5. They want us in Poston, Arizona.
6. ???

This time the trucks took them to a train station where soldiers formed a long line along the platform.

On the train a white man walked through the car

and told them to keep the shades drawn. The train moved slowly. Every so often Sumiko could hear a bang on the windows. Finally she drew aside a shade and saw that a few people were throwing rocks and pebbles. What did they want from her? That was what she didn't understand. What did they want?

The train stopped for a long time, and there seemed to be a furor outside. Finally word had spread through the train that a white man had lain on the tracks to protest the evacuation. As the train started she saw the man being arrested. At first Sumiko had thought they might actually be let go because of this white man. Then when he was arrested, she thought maybe he was crazy. She didn't understand why he had done something that wouldn't change anything at all. The man didn't seem to feel any *haji* at all over his arrest.

Tak-Tak was studying his crickets. Sumiko peered in the box and saw a cricket sitting on a bit of mush Tak-Tak had saved from breakfast. He closed his box with satisfaction.

With the windows shut, the temperature was sweltering, but the same white man who'd told them not to pull up the shades walked through the car and announced that nobody should open the windows. Two people got sick, so it smelled pretty awful in the car. Once a Japanese man hurried through the train calling out, "Is there a doctor in the house?"

Sumiko didn't feel so well herself, but she sat up straight so Tak-Tak wouldn't be scared. When darkness fell outside, the only illumination came from little lights on the sides of the seats. Once in the night Sumiko peeked out and saw strange-shaped trees in a desert. The trees' limbs bent at odd angles, and pronglike leaves shot out from all over.

On the morning of the next day the train pulled into the town of Parker, Arizona. The heat had been growing and growing, like when you light an oven and it keeps getting hotter. One man said cheerfully, "It beats being shot!"

Sumiko and the other Japanese disembarked and saw another line of soldiers to guard them.

"What is that?" Tak-Tak said.

"You mean the soldiers?"

"No . . . it feels weird in the air."

She couldn't help smiling. "It's really, really hot," she said.

"Hot?" he said uncertainly.

Sumiko had never felt anything like it either. Even when she was lighting the fire under the bathtub, the heat was contained in just the area of the fire. Even when they were burning their things, the heat stayed in a small area. But here the heat was everywhere, as if there were fire all around them.

Parker wasn't much of a town. It didn't seem to

consist of anything but a few old stores. White people stood outside the stores, just staring at the Japanese. The staring made Sumiko feel *haji*, as if she'd done something wrong, but also a little anger, because she knew she hadn't done anything wrong. She knew—because Jiichan had once told her so—that the *haji* she felt was from her Japanese side and the anger she felt was from her American side.

Sumiko and her family were headed toward one of several buses lined up in a row. Everybody slid quietly into a seat.

The buses drove off. After that all Sumiko could think was, It's hot. The heat devoured her energy and made her mind so foggy, she could hardly think at all. She wasn't even scared of what might happen next. All she cared about was that it was very, very hot. Still, she knew it was better to feel this hot than to feel the ultimate boredom. She remembered more of what Jiichan had said: "Every time clock tick, closer to ultimate boredom. Have to get to America before lose mind."

The bus driver was a jovial fellow. "You're lucky!" he announced. "It was even hotter last week."

Sumiko looked out the window, though there was nothing to see, just a few old trees and tangled bushes and a lot of light brown dust. Mountains rose in the distance, and a strange, dirty cloud hovered near them. She yawned.

But as they drove the cloud grew larger. She didn't want to alarm Tak-Tak. Bull was sitting in front of her, so she poked him on the shoulder and pointed at the horizon. He squinted out the window.

The cloud was brown and lower to the ground than a normal cloud. Sumiko could see the blue sky above it. It looked like brown, boiling water. Closer to the bus she also saw small swirls of dust rise up from the ground like dancing girls. For a moment she thought the temperature had grown so hot that the air was actually boiling. Maybe that was possible. Something felt good, and Sumiko realized it was that she felt really interested in the brown cloud. She was moving farther away from the ultimate boredom.

The driver called out, "Dust storm to the left! Nothing to worry about. It happens all the time."

Dust! The closer the storm got, the faster it seemed to approach, until suddenly the entire sky darkened and they were in the middle of it. It was hard to tell whether the storm was one big thing or a whole lot of tiny things.

A couple of babies started crying. The driver called out, "Happens all the time, folks! No cause for alarm."

Sumiko had no idea how the driver could see where he was going. Then he stopped, and everyone stirred in their seats. Sumiko couldn't see anything outside.

"We're stuck," said the driver. "We'll have to wait it out." The driver sat back and drank from a Thermos. He whistled tunes, and every so often he called out, "No cause for alarm!"

After a while Sumiko felt claustrophobic. She wanted to scream and escape this bus. She concentrated as hard as she could on keeping the scream inside her.

In about an hour, when the dust storm died down, the driver said, "All able-bodied men are going to have to help get the bus unstuck."

All the men got up immediately. The women got off to lighten the load for the men. The other buses had also stopped at various places along the road. Some of the men were covered head to toe in dust. They looked as if they'd jumped into a vat of brown paint. Sumiko couldn't help smiling when she saw Tak-Tak hurry to the back of the bus to push alongside the men.

When the men had freed the bus, everyone got back on.

Nothing seemed real. The world outside was brown. The sky was sort of tan. All the men were brown; even Sumiko in her previously mint green school dress was brown. Everything in the world was brown and very hot.

14

A COUPLE OF HOURS LATER THEY PASSED A GROUPING of hundreds of plain barracks that looked so familiar, Sumiko thought for a moment someone had transported the racetrack assembly center to the desert. She thought a desert was supposed to be full of sand dunes, but this desert was filled with dry bushes and dry trees growing in dry dirt. Tractors moved like huge dirt-eating animals in the distance, and in other places men seemed to be leveling the ground.

"Is that a chain gang?" she asked Bull. She had seen a movie once with a chain gang.

"I don't know," he said.

"They're digging irrigation ditches," Ichiro told her.

"In the middle of the desert?" Sumiko asked.

"There must be a water source somewhere."

Sumiko couldn't see any signs of water. Then she caught a glimpse of what seemed like a mirage: a lush green field.

Several men on the other side of the bus jumped out of their seats to see. One man leaned over Sumiko and squinted.

"Looks like beans," he said.

The bus drove past a second, smaller group of barracks. The driver announced, "You'll all be staying in Camp Three." He drove a couple of miles more and pulled up to a last group of barracks. The road didn't extend beyond this last group. It stopped right where the bus stopped. The driver explained that Poston—officially called the Colorado River Relocation Center—was divided into three camps that would ultimately hold several thousand occupants each, for a total of more than seventeen thousand. "Camp Three is the smallest one. Some people say it's the wildest, but that's just a rumor. They're all the same."

Everybody got out and carried their things into the camp. A few *Nikkei* greeted them, but Sumiko didn't see many people. She turned this way and that but didn't see much of anything except barracks and desert. At least the assembly center in California had seemed like it was in the middle of *somewhere*.

Something started buzzing louder and louder—and then even louder. Everyone from the bus started muttering and looking at the sky. A few called out in alarm. A plane swooped down toward the camp. It looked as if it were going to dive right into them! They were going to die! Sumiko felt herself being thrown to the ground. The sound of the plane grew deafening and then subsided. She lifted her head and saw the plane flying away.

Bull was lying next to her, one arm around her and the other around Tak-Tak. Some other newcomers were lying on the ground. She heard laughing and saw several people smiling. She got up and didn't even bother to dust off, since her dress was already a disaster.

A man said, "That's a pilot from an American air base. They just buzz us to harass us. We're supposed to get their number and report them."

"What number?" said Ichiro.

The man shrugged. "Who knows? We're not allowed to keep binoculars."

Tak-Tak started crying; he had skinned an elbow. Bull looked exhausted. "Sumiko, take care of him."

Just then another man called out, "Ich!" Sumiko recognized one of Ichiro's friends. Like Ichiro, this man was formerly a party boy in fancy clothes, but now he looked like any other farmer in plain pants and shirt.

"Mas!" called out Ichiro. They shook hands. Bull joined them as they huddled together and spoke too quietly for Sumiko to hear.

Sumiko hugged Tak-Tak as he cried. "You have to act like a big boy," she said.

"I don't want to," he said, crying even louder. Dust covered the lenses of his glasses. Sumiko tried to clean the dust off but ended up just smearing it all over.

Sumiko's family was checked in by *Nikkei* volunteers. The volunteers were rather cheerful and told Ichiro that they should "try to make the best of it." The family was assigned a barrack and sent to another barrack for a quick checkup by a doctor. Then they were sent outside.

Sumiko noticed that there was dust everywhere, and it seemed lighter than air. As if there were no gravity, the surface of the ground lifted with every step or soft breeze. Tak-Tak coughed and coughed. Sumiko wiped the middle of his face with his shirt and tied his handkerchief around his nose and mouth. Underneath the dust he looked gray and pathetic. His skin looked like a mask in the middle of all the brown dust.

"Put down your things, Tak-Tak. I'll come for them later," Bull said. "Come on, climb on my back."

Tak-Tak seemed so weak, he could hardly hold on

to Bull's back. But he smiled a little bit as he leaned his cheek on Bull's neck.

Bull carried a couple of suitcases in his hands as well as carrying Tak-Tak on his back. Sumiko struggled to keep up.

The barrack they were assigned to was at the far end of the camp. As Sumiko trudged across the ground, dust rose like flour with every step. Small groups of kids sat in the shade with wet towels on their heads.

"Welcome to paradise!" one of them called out. To Sumiko's surprise, here and there she saw signs of home: curtains in a window, some gardens, even a few partially completed ponds. Sumiko wondered, What will they fill those ponds with—dust?

Each of the barracks was twenty feet by one hundred feet, with four families housed in each barrack. There were fourteen barracks to a block, and each block had a mess hall and a men's and a women's latrine, as well as one barrack for "recreation." It was a lot like the assembly center except for a few differences:

1. It was ten times hotter.
2. It felt like a leper colony because it was so isolated.
3. It was permanent.

They reached their barrack and the others went in. Sumiko stood outside, examining a homemade cage about four feet by four feet holding several rattlesnakes. Sumiko tried to figure out why anyone would keep snakes in a cage.

"Sumiko, get out of this sun!" Auntie called, and Sumiko stepped through the door.

There was nothing at all inside their room. Sumiko could hear people talking from next door. There were big knotholes in the wood; something that looked like a scorpion sat in one. She screamed. Bull saw what she'd screamed at and poked the scorpion out with his foot before stomping it so hard, the whole barrack shook.

A man with a patch over one eye stuck his head inside. "Everything okay here?"

"It was a *scorpion*," said Sumiko.

"Don't worry. They bite, but they're not the fatal kind," said the man with the patch. He leaned in and stuck out his hand aggressively. "I'm Mr. Moto." Bull and Ichiro shook his hand.

Ichiro looked furious. "We have children here," he said. "We can't live with scorpions!"

Mr. Moto laughed and said, "Tell that to the scorpions." But he saw how serious Ichiro was and stopped laughing. "Well, let me know if you need anything."

"Who do we complain to about the scorpion?" Ichiro asked.

Mr. Moto looked surprised. "Well, nobody," he said. "They live here." He paused. "Okay, bye." He disappeared from the doorway.

Sumiko gaped at the pile of gunk that had been a scorpion a minute earlier. Ichiro snapped at her, "Clean that up."

Sumiko stepped into the dust outside and saw an old woman walking slowly down the way. *"Sumimasen!"* Sumiko called. She hurried to the woman. "Do you know where a mop is?"

"One mop each block. Maybe Mura-san have." The woman indicated a barrack and continued walking slowly away.

Sumiko peered into the barrack. Inside were tables, chairs, pretty curtains, bedspreads, and a rug. A woman was mopping. *"Sumimasen,"* Sumiko said. "We're new, and I was wondering if I could use the mop when you finish."

"Take it," the woman said tiredly. "Here, you can borrow my bucket, too."

Sumiko brought the mop and bucket back to her barrack. Tak-Tak was kneeling, fascinated, over the squished scorpion. Seeing Tak-Tak's face so alert made Sumiko actually feel happy that there was a dead scorpion on the floor. "The guts have yellow in them," Tak-Tak said. He lifted his glasses and looked more closely. "There's a piece of blue, too."

"Careful, it's poison. Did you touch it?"

"I don't know. Sumiko, can I have the scorpion?"

"No."

"Please?" He gave her his best cute look.

"No."

His face fell. "Well, here. Mr. Moto said to give you a rag."

She sprinkled dust on the scorpion to sop up some of the liquid, then wrapped the scorpion in the rag.

Auntie said Bull had gone to get their cots. Dust covered everything. Just curious, Sumiko stamped her foot and watched dust rise into the air.

Auntie shrieked, "Stop that, are you crazy?!"

The way she shrieked made Sumiko wonder whether Auntie herself was crazy. But Sumiko apologized.

Ichiro surveyed the room. "I'll have to make some chairs and a table," he said. He glanced at Sumiko holding the rag. "Haven't you thrown that thing out yet? Get busy." He walked out. Sumiko wrinkled her nose at Tak-Tak. "Everybody's in a bad mood," she whispered.

Sumiko mopped until another woman came in to ask for the mop, and Sumiko gladly gave it up.

But after she had given it up, she didn't know what to do with herself. She just stood outside looking around. Her family was in the last barrack in the last block of the last camp. There was no fence, but, Sumiko realized, there was nowhere to go, either. She'd seen a guard gate when they drove by the first camp, but she didn't see one here. She knew what would happen if someone tried to escape into the desert. They would die of thirst.

Sumiko stepped away from the barrack. She didn't know what was considered the border of the camp. She took a couple of steps out, then a couple more, then a couple more. She felt nervous. She saw something in the distance growing closer. At first she thought it might be a car, but then she saw it was a horse, and finally she realized it was a man on a horse. The man rode until he was only about a hundred feet from her. He was an Indian man with long hair. Sumiko looked around. Was she just imagining this man? He seemed to nod at her before he rode away.

A snake hissed at Sumiko from the cage behind her. "Oh, quiet," said a deep voice, and Sumiko turned to see Mr. Moto frowning at the snake. To Sumiko he said, "We'll eat him later."

"Sorry?"

"I said, we'll eat him later. You'll be begging me for a bite, you'll see."

She studied the man. She wasn't sure whether he was kidding. He winked, or at least she thought that's what it meant when he closed his only eye and squeezed it shut.

"Mark my words," he said.

At dinnertime Sumiko got in line with her family and let the kitchen staff fill her rice bowl, plate, and cup. The cup held milk; she wasn't sure what was on the plate and in the bowl. It wasn't rice in the bowl, it was . . . something else. Something mushy.

Kids were eating with one another instead of with their families; many of the tables seemed arranged by age rather than family units. She looked around with interest. There were even a couple of tables with kids about her age.

Sumiko was starving until Bull said, "It looks like beef tongue in tomato sauce."

Ichiro smiled balefully. "And what's this?" He lifted something mushy from his bowl and let it ooze off his fork and plop back into the bowl.

Someone from the next table said, "Mashed potatoes."

It didn't look like any mashed potatoes Sumiko had ever seen. For one thing, mashed potatoes were white. She thought curiously of Mr. Moto's rattlesnake and tried to imagine what snake might taste like.

She hardly ate anything at dinner. And she didn't even wait to be excused by Auntie. She just grabbed Tak-Tak and rushed with him to Mr. Moto's home. Mr. Moto was already outside frying his snake on a little stove he'd made from a big can and some wood chips. He smiled at her. "I'll bet you're ready for this, aren't you?" He handed her a sliver of meat on a fork. The snake was pretty good with a little *shoyu* and ginger. It tasted like *unagi*: eel. Not a strong taste and not bad at all. She considered further and thought maybe it tasted more like the dark meat of a turkey. Tak-Tak loved it. He said he wanted to eat it raw.

As they ate, Mr. Moto told them that he and his twenty-year-old son had been in this camp just a week. Sumiko was surprised. He seemed like an old hand. He looked at them, evaluating. "Can you kids work?"

"I can," Sumiko said.

Tak-Tak said defensively, "I can work too!"

That's how they found themselves carrying buckets of water from the latrines to the barrack. Mr. Moto was trying to soak the ground so the dirt would be softer and he could start building a garden. Lugging water from the latrines was hard work. On the one hand, it made Sumiko feel useful; but on the other hand, it made her feel ridiculous because it was futile. Why drag water through a desert? What kind of garden could you grow here?

That night many of the kids, including Sumiko, slept with their cots under the stars. It was cooler outside, and the night breeze made you feel almost less than hot. The leaves from the surrounding mesquite trees hit dryly against one another. The moon had never seemed brighter.

People were talking, but Sumiko's mind drifted. To her this camp was entirely different from the assembly center camp. This camp felt final. This is where she would live maybe the next ten years of her life, depending on how long the war lasted. And there was something else about this camp, but she couldn't put her finger on it. Just as Sumiko sometimes told Tak-Tak to search his mind for the sleep in his head, she searched her own mind, though she was uncertain what she was searching for.

She got the feeling that a majority of the other *Nikkei* seemed to understand and accept what was happening to them. Maybe some of them saw this place the same way they saw a tornado or an earthquake. You wouldn't get mad at a tornado, would you? For Sumiko, her whole life, from the day she was born, had been a lesson in how to change your lot by accepting it and learning from it.

But she yearned for the farm. An hour earlier, on the farm, she and her family might have been listening to the radio, as they sometimes did in the evenings. Jiichan was somewhat hard of hearing, so the radio was always turned up pretty loud. But there were no radios allowed in camp. She smiled as she remembered how mad Jiichan got if anybody dared to suggest the radio was too loud. "What you try to say?" he would demand. "You try to say I have old-man ears?"

Sumiko thought about the *kusabana* and wondered what had become of them. She hoped that someone had rented the farm soon after they left and that the flowers were thriving.

Bull had already built Tak-Tak a new cage for his crickets—he'd found screen from a scrap pile and made the cage his priority after he'd fetched the cots. Tak-Tak had brought the crickets outside for the night, and their chirping filled the air. A couple of bats swooped through the camp, and at one point Sumiko heard sounds of shouting—someone had been bitten by a scorpion. She kept thinking something was crawling on her and she would jump up, but there would be nothing there. Finally she settled down. She heard laughing as a group of boys ran down the block, right past Sumiko's cot and beyond the imaginary boundary of the camp.

A huge, beautiful moth fluttered around the cot and then flew away. Sumiko's mother had been named Mayu, which meant "cocoon" but implied "nurturing" and also "transformation." Jiichan always said that a larva changed itself by staying very still. The larva went from being the ugliest thing in the world to the most beautiful.

Sumiko thought about how for the past couple of years she'd dreamed that she would go to college and get a business degree so she could run her flower shop. She knew she was just a farm girl, but deep within herself she believed that every flower she disbudded, every dish she washed, every day the girls snubbed her, every morning she woke at dawn brought her closer to her dream, to her transformation from farm girl to flower shop owner. She did not want a big flower shop, she just wanted to be surrounded by flowers every day for the rest of her life. She wanted to fill out invoices and arrange her display window. She wanted to name her first daughter Hanako, which meant "flower child."

But now, lying on that cot in the middle of the desert, surrounded by moths and bats and scorpions, it seemed to Sumiko that the flower shop was no longer within reach for her. Her dream was gone, and she didn't know what would take its place.

15

THE SUN BATTERED SUMIKO'S FACE WHEN SHE WOKE UP. She tried to open her eyes but couldn't. Last night they'd been so irritated by the dust that mucous had oozed out of them. The mucous had apparently dried, and now Sumiko had to pry open her eyes with her fingers.

Everybody else who'd slept outside had already gotten up and taken their cots in. Sumiko went to stand in the line at the shower. The showerheads were arranged in a row, with no partitions. One woman carried a flimsy folding screen made of crooked wood and cloth. She folded the screen around while she showered. A couple of women took showers in their brassieres and bloomers. Even though people avoided one another's eyes, Sumiko felt quite shy and took her shower in her underclothes. Afterward she just put her regular clothes on over her wet things.

When she got back to her barrack, she saw several boys carrying fishing poles. There was one girl with them. She said they were walking down to the Colorado River to fish. "Come with us!" she called out. "There's nothing else to do."

Sumiko peered inside her barrack and saw Tak-Tak in bed. Ichiro and Bull were off somewhere. Auntie had just gotten up. Before they'd all been relocated, Sumiko had never known Auntie to sleep past sunrise. Sumiko asked, "Auntie, can I go down to the Colorado River with some kids?"

Auntie looked up. The way she looked made Sumiko nervous. Auntie's eyes seemed to hold hints of the ultimate boredom. "No, it's dangerous," Auntie said lethargically.

"They're all going."

"No.

Sumiko went outside and told the kids she couldn't go. One of the boys laughed. "You don't have to ask for permission out here. You can just do whatever you want!" The boys hurried off, but the girl lingered. She was a skinny girl with a shiny face.

"My name is Sachi Shibata."

"I'm Sumiko Matsuda." Before the war she and

Tak-Tak had gone by their father's name, Yamaguchi. But to avoid confusion in camp, they now went by Uncle's name.

"My father owned the biggest potato farm in America, in Palm Springs," Sachi said. "We used to be millionaires."

Sumiko hesitated; that didn't ring true because she thought the biggest Japanese potato farmers were the Ito family from the Northwest. "Really?" she said.

"Yes, we owned thirty horses. One of them won the Kentucky Derby."

Sumiko could use a friend, even a friend who lied. "We had a flower farm," Sumiko said.

"Have you seen the Camp Three farm?"

"No."

"Come on, I'll show you."

Sumiko looked toward her barrack. She should tell Auntie that she was leaving. But she thought of what the boy had said.

Sachi read her mind. "Nobody listens to their parents in camp. Come on!"

So they hurried off. They stopped at a kitchen, where Sachi sweetly asked one of the cooks for two cups of ice. He gave her the cups, and she handed one to Sumiko. They ate ice and walked across the camp. Here and there in the morning sun she noticed men and a few women working on gardens outside their barracks. One man was even planting a tree. She couldn't imagine where he'd gotten a tree.

At the edge of camp Sumiko saw what looked like another mirage. But it really *was* a bean field, with beans hanging from posts and so opulent that they seemed impossible. Judging from the colors of the flowers—lilac and scarlet—there appeared to be two different kinds of bean plants. Here and there a couple of string beans hung from a vine. The posts were shaped into upside-down V's several feet high. The irrigation ditches beside them were narrow and utterly dry. She figured the beans had been watered that morning but were already drying out in the desert sun.

In the distance tractors roared as men leveled the land. Sumiko had seen land leveled many times. As Sachi and Sumiko watched, two white men in white shirts came up and stood nearby, surveying the activity.

The shorter of the two seemed to be admiring the beans. "I told you so—look at those beans!" he said. "The Japs sure have a knack for growing things." He ignored Sumiko and Sachi. Sumiko had been ignored many times before by *hakujin*, so this was nothing new to her.

"What else have they got to do?" the taller man replied. He seemed irritated. "Let me tell you something. We've found it's easier to get our Indians to work than your Japs."

"Your Indians are getting paid a lot more."

"Why shouldn't they be?"

The men moved away, still talking.

"Let's get a closer look!" said Sumiko.

They walked into the bean field, and it was like walking into a different world. They stood right in the middle of the field, surrounded by green. Suddenly Sachi hissed, "Shh! Hide!"

"What?"

"Hide!"

They slipped into a tunnel formed by the way the beans grew over the posts. Sachi and Sumiko peeked out.

"It's Indian boys," Sachi whispered. "They're not supposed to be in our camp. If they catch us, we'll get scalped." Sumiko crouched lower but couldn't stop herself from peeking out.

There were three boys, maybe Sumiko's age or a little older. They were looking around, sometimes gazing afar at the men working, other times examining the plants close by. One of them was chewing gum, and he had a scarf tied around his head. The other two were lanky and looked like twins. "After they scalp us, they'll cut off our fingers and boil them," Sachi added. Sumiko's heart pounded in her ears.

The boys moved closer to where Sachi and Sumiko were hiding. One of the lanky boys said, "My brother said the Japs are all farmers."

"They're wasteful," said the boy chewing gum. "They throw food out all the time!"

Suddenly Sumiko heard a rattlesnake right near the tunnel. Sachi screamed, and they both pushed through the vines squealing. Sumiko tripped and found herself on her rear end a foot away from the snake.

It rose in the air and hissed.

"Walk back slowly. *Slowly.* It doesn't want to hurt you," a calm voice said. Someone lifted her onto her feet and took hold of her shoulders and walked slowly backward with her.

Once they were far enough away from the snake, Sumiko turned around and found herself facing the Indian boy who was chewing gum. He had short hair and wide, muscular shoulders. He shook his head. "Were you just going to sit there until it bit you?" He seemed annoyed.

She opened her mouth to answer but couldn't think of a thing to say. She'd never talked to an Indian before. She saw Sachi running off.

The boy looked at her, evaluating. She saw his eyes flicker momentarily, but she wasn't sure what that meant.

The other boys walked up and stared at her. They seemed fascinated, kind of like when Tak-Tak was studying the scorpion.

"She doesn't look so dangerous," said one of the lanky boys.

The other said, "If they think you're going to kill them, they stick a sword in their stomach before you can do it. I read that."

"Does she talk?"

"Of course she talks."

"How do you know?"

"Unless she's a mute."

"Maybe she doesn't speak English."

The boy with the scarf tilted his head at her. "She's scared!"

"I'm not scared!" Sumiko said indignantly, although she felt more scared of them than any white people she'd ever been around.

They stepped back a bit when she spoke, as if they were surprised.

Another boy appeared from seemingly out of nowhere. "Come on, I gotta get home," he called out.

"Hold on, Hook," said the boy with the scarf. He blew a bubble as he continued to study Sumiko. The fourth boy came up. A hook stuck out from his left arm where a hand should have been. Sumiko was surprised to hear this boy called "Hook." It would be like calling Mr. Moto "One Eye." If a Japanese person had a hook for a hand, you would act like the hook wasn't even there and get all embarrassed if you got caught staring at it.

The new boy looked at her curiously, then set his right hand on the shoulder of the boy with the scarf.

"Come on, Frank, they're going to be here for the whole war."

Frank started to walk away, then turned back to Sumiko. "Why don't you people go back where you came from and leave our reservation alone?" he said.

Sumiko felt too scared to answer, and the boys sauntered off without looking back. She walked home by herself. Sachi was waiting in the doorway of Sumiko's barrack. She ran out.

"Are you sure the Indians didn't follow you?"

The thought hadn't occurred to Sumiko. She turned around, but all she could see were barracks and desert. "Are we on a reservation?" she asked.

"Of course," said Sachi. "That's why we're in constant danger."

"But where do they live?" In town when they'd first arrived at the camp, she'd seen only white people.

"They live everywhere, silly. They're *Indians*. They hide at night. If we don't behave, they'll kidnap your family when it gets dark. You're in special danger because you live at the camp border." Then Sachi seemed to tire of her own lies. "Well, bye."

"Bye," said Sumiko, only half listening. She stared into the desert and wondered, Where *do* the Indians live?

16

AFTER A FEW DAYS SUMIKO REALIZED THAT SHE DIDN'T know what to do with herself. She remembered that sometimes at the farm she'd wished she had more time so she could go out with the friends she didn't have. Now she was rich in time but had nothing to do. Other people, like Ichiro and Bull, immediately got busy—Bull laying foundation for irrigation canals and Ichiro driving the regular shuttle bus between Camps One, Two, and Three. The government paid them a fraction of what they might get paid outside for such work. But as Bull said, "Money is money." Even Tak-Tak found a group of marble-playing boys to hang around with. And Auntie, who'd seemed so lethargic at first, joined a sewing club and immediately made pretty curtains for the barrack.

During the evenings Mr. Moto would work on his garden or his carving. Many of the Japanese men spent much of their time carving wood they gathered in the mountains. Every so often some of them would walk to the mountains or even drive one of the tractors there. But nobody ever tried to escape.

Sometimes Sumiko just sat around watching Mr. Moto carve wood or dig in his soon-to-be garden. He was one of the minority of *Nikkei* who were not farmers.

"Mr. Moto?" said Sumiko one day a week after she'd arrived. He was digging a big, round hole about three feet deep. She knew it wasn't her place to comment, but she didn't understand what he was doing. "If you're going to plant something there, you don't need to dig a big hole like that."

He seemed a little insulted. "I'm building a pond," he said.

"Oh!"

"I had a pond garden in my old home, so I thought I'd do the same thing here, next to my vegetables."

He kept digging, ignoring her. He probably wanted her to leave him alone. But an idea had occurred to her. "Mr. Moto?"

He looked up, wiping sweat from his face and, in the process, smearing dirt over his only eye.

"Are you going to plant any flowers?"

"I don't have any flower seeds," he said.

"I have some. They're the most beautiful flowers in the world!" she blurted out. Of course, she hadn't actually seen Uncle's Sumiko Strain, but she figured his hard work *must* be beautiful.

Mr. Moto nodded thoughtfully. "I was thinking of only vegetables. But I'll tell you what. Let me sleep on it."

Sumiko was surprised at how disappointed she felt that he needed to sleep on it. "Okay," she said. He went back to digging. On the farm she had never done work that required a lot of physical strength, like digging in hard ground. So now she felt she needed Mr. Moto's help. Otherwise, she could have simply planted her own garden—that is, if she ever found the energy.

Sumiko felt the ultimate boredom closing in on her. The ultimate boredom wasn't dread of the next year or of what the government might do next; it was dread of your own mind, dread of the next day, the next hour, the next minute. You could lose your mind at any time. Like one morning, for no good reason, Sumiko actually stomped on a butterfly that landed in the dust. After she moved her foot, she saw the squished butterfly and wondered what had come over her. She hadn't thought about it beforehand, but had just suddenly stomped on the poor butterfly. She figured maybe she'd had a sudden attack of the ultimate boredom, and then when she'd seen the dead butterfly she snapped out of it.

One day Sumiko took the shuttle bus to Camp One to visit her father's brother, Uncle Kenzo, on his birthday. Auntie made her do that; he was a grouch, and she'd never been close to him. So that kept her busy for a little while. She just sat in his room with his glum family for a few hours, then returned to Camp Three. On the bus to Camp One she'd been surprised to see how many gardens were already springing up all over Poston.

Later that day Sumiko was so bored, she just flopped to the ground right outside her barrack and didn't move. A butterfly fluttered over her. She wondered if the butterfly were actually the ultimate boredom in disguise. She wondered whether it planned to flutter and flutter and then *strike*! She wondered if maybe she had already lost her mind. It was possible.

Sumiko felt so lazy that a few days ago instead of writing Jiichan and Uncle an actual letter, she just sent them some lists she scribbled around the edges of old copies of the *Poston Chronicle*—the camp newspaper run by camp residents. In return, she received a letter from Jiichan that was written in a circle around the margin of a sheet of paper.

Dear Sumiko,

1. *We don't deserve real letter?*
2. *You so busy you can't write in good penmanship?*
3. *You must be very busy.*
4. *Jiichan and Uncle*

But even that didn't affect Sumiko. She just stuck the letter in her luggage and didn't think about it again.

Her only pleasure, if it could be called a "pleasure," was lying outside at night under the stars. She liked to listen as people from her barrack lay on their cots outside and talked. In the background the wind would agitate the mesquite and send dust into the night like ghosts rising from the ground.

One night Mr. Moto told about the rolling green hills of the Japanese countryside. He'd been born in Seattle but educated in Japan. He said that if America sent him back to Japan, he would buy a rice farm in the country. He'd owned a grocery store at the time of the evacuation, but his parents had been rice farmers. "Before the evacuation I sold the store and my house in a package deal for one thousand dollars, even though I paid four thousand for the house in 1940."

Another man said, "Ah, *shikata ga nai.*"

Sumiko heard that phrase all the time lately.

For instance, the previous night Mr. Moto had told Sumiko that he'd fallen on a rake as a boy. That's how he'd lost an eye. He'd said, *"Shikata ga nai."* That meant "This cannot be helped." Once when Sumiko had asked Jiichan how sad it had made him when her mother died, he'd said, *"Shikata ga nai."* When your house burned down, when someone you loved died, when your heart was broken, when you suffered any tragedy, but also when you merely broke a toenail, that's what the Japanese said.

This cannot be helped.

After telling everyone about his house, Mr. Moto got out of his cot and leaned into his doorway. "Son?"

"What?"

"Don't you want to be outside? Everybody is talking."

"I'm trying to sleep, Dad."

So Mr. Moto returned to lie in his cot. Sumiko rarely saw Mr. Moto's son. She guessed he was just in the mood to be alone.

Mr. Moto started talking about Poston. He said he'd once wanted to be a teacher, so he liked to give little lectures once in a while. "Poston is in the Sonoran Desert," he said. "It's one of the hottest areas in the country. There used to be just a few buildings around here, but now the camp is the third-largest town in Arizona."

"How did you find that out?" Sumiko asked. "I thought there are no maps in camp."

Mr. Moto pointed to his head. "They can keep the maps out of Poston but not out of my head. I know my geography."

"You would have made a good teacher," Sumiko said. "You—"

A man suddenly snapped, "Quiet!"

And Sumiko shut her mouth instantly. She knew an *inu* had just walked into view at the end of the barrack. *Inu* meant "dog," but people used it to mean "dirty dog" or "snitch" who worked for the white administration to spy on other *Nikkei*.

The man continued to stand there, and one by one people dragged their cots inside. Sumiko was disappointed—she liked lying outside. But she dragged her cot into her barrack.

She couldn't sleep because of the heat. After a while she heard a dust storm rising, and then she heard grunting and pounding from outside. For a second she wasn't sure she heard the grunting, but the noises grew louder and louder. She was torn between jumping out of bed and staying as still as she could. Sweat poured from her forehead. Somehow she knew exactly what was happening, even though she had never before heard the sick sound of a man getting beaten. She knew it was the *inu*.

Finally she got up. "Stay there!" Ichiro and Bull ordered at the same time. They ran outside. Sumiko jumped up anyway and looked out the door with

Auntie and Tak-Tak. About forty feet away she could make out several men kicking another man. The dust made it seem like she was watching through a veil.

The man getting beaten was named Yamada. Everybody believed he was an *inu*. He probably *was* an *inu*. A woman had told Yamada that she secretly owned a camera, and the next day her barrack had been searched and the camera confiscated.

Ichiro and Bull returned to the room.

"Should we help him?" said Sumiko.

Ichiro shook his head. "Absolutely not." Sumiko turned to Bull, but he just got back in bed and lay there. Sumiko wondered whether his eyes were wide open like her own.

Yamada groaned so loudly, Sumiko could hear him clearly. She heard talking, crying, shouting, pleading. She couldn't stand it!

"Bull, I can't stand it!" she said.

"I know," he said.

Guilt filled her soul. Sumiko knew in her heart that Yamada was an *inu*. Some of the *inu* were very friendly and smiled when they saw you. Sumiko didn't mind the people who were unhappy at their treatment, and she didn't mind the people who thought they should try to make the best of things. But like everybody else, she didn't like the *inu*. Still, the sound of Yamada's groans made her feel like groaning herself.

It seemed they beat him forever. Sumiko felt an ache grow in her stomach. She just stood in the center of the room willing herself not to be there. I'm not here. I'm out there. I'm not here. And for a moment it came true, and she was at the farm again, watching the white cheesecloth billow over the flowers they had worked so hard to grow, watching birds fly above the cloth, and watching her family—all of them—work peacefully in the weedflowers.

Then the beating ended. And there was silence. The groaning stopped, and even the wind stopped.

Silence, finally, silence.

17

SUMIKO READ IN THE *CHRONICLE* THAT POSTON was the only *Nikkei* relocation center administered by the Office of Indian Affairs. Maybe that was why security seemed rather lax here. Supposedly, the other relocation centers were run by the War Relocation Authority. The camps for *Issei* like Jiichan and Uncle were run by the Department of Justice and were more like prisons.

Before long you could do many things in the town of Poston that you could do in any town. You could sit at the movies (if you'd made your own chair), get a job cooking food (at a mess hall), drive a truck (but not too far), build buildings (only in the camp), dig irrigation ditches, build basketball courts or baseball diamonds, play on a baseball or basketball team, farm, deliver mail, work at a store, fight fires, join the government, join a gang, and join clubs. Working at least kept you busy, even though you got paid much less than you would make outside for the same work. Some camp residents kept busy running for office and fighting over political control of the camps. Ultimately, the white administration made the major decisions, but the residents also got a say.

Every day the *Chronicle* told of dances in the block recreation halls; new clubs or classes for gardening, sewing, learning English, and many other subjects; tournaments for marbles, basketball, baseball, and other sports; job offers; elections and meetings; items for sale; and so on.

One thing the newspaper didn't cover was the war. Nobody had the least idea who was winning. Some people thought Japan was winning, and others thought the United States was winning. One man whom nobody listened to much said that the war in Europe was just as important as the war in the Pacific. But nobody talked much about Germany. It was always Japan this and Japan that. Ichiro said the government didn't want them knowing anything about what was going on in the war.

The grown-ups in camp complained all the time about how wild the kids were getting. Sachi and some other girls sometimes stole candy bars from the canteen.

And some of the boys had stolen a pig and put it in an *inu*'s barrack. Sumiko had seen them giggling maniacally as they ran through camp carrying the squealing animal.

The camp was hot and awful and ugly and boring, but because it was "permanent," Sumiko started to get used to it. And she found she kind of liked being bad. She wasn't *bad* bad, but when she didn't feel like it, she didn't sit with Auntie and Tak-Tak during meals. And she stayed out late a few times, just sitting around with Sachi and the other kids. Some of them smoked, but the one time she tried it, she got so sick, two boys needed to carry her home.

One day as Sumiko walked with Sachi, her friend suddenly cried out, "Now!" She fell upon the vegetable garden they had been walking by and began pulling up carrots.

"What are we doing?" Sumiko cried out.

Sachi ran off calling back, "Goody Two-shoes!"

Sumiko knew how good fresh carrots tasted, but still, it was wrong to steal them like that.

Sumiko walked alone back to her barrack. Nobody was around. Even Mr. Moto had gone somewhere. But she noticed a letter for herself from Uncle on the tablecloth.

Sumiko,

I am writing this for Jiichan. He said to tell you he can't write himself because he is very busy, as he says you must be. (He says not to tell you that he is being sarcastic.) He says he knows you are not becoming namakemono. *He says he hopes you are behaving well and doing whatever your aunt tells you. He hopes you have started a garden that would make him proud.*

We are well enough here in North Dakota. It's already [this part was censored]. By the way, please thank your aunt for the socks she managed to send. I hate to ask for more, since I know conditions cannot [censored]. But can you please tell Auntie that if she finds money to spare, we will need better boots and Jiichan would like a better coat. Tell her not to worry if she cannot find the money.

Please take care. We may be moved to [censored].

Oh, and Jiichan says to send you the enclosed blank sheet of paper. He says there must be a paper shortage in Poston, since you are using old newspapers to write on. He says he wonders where your aunt is getting the blank paper she writes to us on.

Much love,
Uncle Hatsumi

Sumiko tucked the letter in her luggage. *Namakemono* meant "lazybones." She didn't think she was a lazybones. It was just that there was nothing to do. The letter didn't make her feel like working. It made her feel tired. She lay down on her cot. Her uncle and grandfather would die of cold, and she would die of heat. And then, she believed, the rest of America would be satisfied.

Sumiko tried to lie there and feel lazy, but finally she got up and drew all of her six dollars from under the mattress and left it on the table with Uncle's letter and a note to Auntie, telling her to use the money for the coat and boots. The heat that day was astounding. She fell asleep, and when she woke up, the money, the letter, and the note were gone. But Tak-Tak was waiting for her to wake up.

"I'm bored," he said. "Why can't we go to summer school?"

Sumiko had always felt school took her away from the farm. But now she wished they would start a school in camp soon. There were rumors that schools would be built and that schoolbooks and teachers would arrive eventually, but nothing ever happened.

"Where are your new friends who play marbles?" Sumiko asked.

"They say I'm not good enough to play with them."

"Oh." Tak-Tak seemed awfully pathetic when he was bored. "All right, let's go see what Sachi is doing."

But Sachi wasn't home. So Sumiko decided to take her brother to the bean fields. A cook gave them two precious cups of ice, and they walked down to the fields. Sumiko brought a pencil and her receipt book.

When they got to the bean tunnels, Sumiko checked for snakes before they slipped under the vines. Tak-Tak sucked on his ice while she made out a couple of receipts. One dollar for roses. Two dollars for arrangement. Someday when she ran out of pages in the book, she planned to erase everything and start over again. But writing out receipts wasn't as much fun as it once had been, when she'd really believed she might own a flower shop one day. So she set the book aside and lay on her back chewing ice. She could see bits of the blue sky through the vines.

Suddenly she became aware of someone else in the tunnel. She shot up. Tak-Tak was staring at the Indian boy, Frank. He was chewing gum again, and he still wore a scarf around his head. Sumiko knew Sachi had lied about the finger boiling, but she still felt scared of this boy.

He peered into Tak-Tak's cup.

"What is that?"

Tak-Tak just stared at him. "It's ice," said Sumiko.

Frank blew a bubble and popped it. "They give *you* ice?" he said.

"Why shouldn't they?"

"I'm not the one who bombed Pearl Harbor."

"You killed Custer," she shot back. She'd learned that in school.

He blew another bubble and popped it. "Don't think you can insult me, 'cause you can't." He glanced with interest at Sumiko's cup but then pulled aside some vines to peer outside. "Who's in charge of the irrigation?"

"An engineer."

"Jap?"

She frowned. "We don't use that word." Then she didn't feel scared of Frank any longer but, rather, annoyed. She answered his question anyway. "The man in charge is white."

He looked at her coldly. Then he seemed to soften, but just a bit. Sumiko saw him glance again at her cup.

"Haven't you seen ice before?" she asked.

"Of course I have." He laughed at the stupidity of her question.

Sumiko sipped at some of the melting ice. He watched intently. "Well, why are you staring, then?" she said.

"I'm not."

Tak-Tak said, "He can have mine."

Frank turned to Tak-Tak and said, surprisingly gently, "No." He pulled a piece of gum from his pocket and threw it to Tak-Tak. Tak-Tak smiled.

To Sumiko, Frank said, "You know anything about the irrigation?"

"My cousin's pouring concrete for the main ditch. They're extending it."

"Really? You from a farm family?"

"Yes, we grew flowers."

"Flowers?" he said. He seemed surprised, even disdainful.

"Uh-huh. You know, like they sell at the store."

"You can make a living from that?" he asked dubiously.

"Of course. What do you mean?"

He shrugged. "I don't know. I never thought of flowers growing on a farm. Why didn't you grow food?"

She hesitated. "Do you really want to know?" Before her camp experiences nobody had asked her many questions about her family.

He seemed confused. "Of course I want to know. That's why I asked."

Well! Sumiko scarcely knew where to start. From when Uncle was a boy? From Uncle's wedding day? She had heard the story many times.

"Before my uncle got married," she said, "he was living in a boardinghouse for bachelors from Fukushima Prefecture in Japan. Prefectures are like states. Anyway, another bachelor who had decided to return to Fukushima asked whether my uncle wanted to marry his sister, who was born in the United States." Sumiko took a breath. Frank looked like he was still listening, so she continued. "The bachelor had been using hired help to run a flower farm, which my uncle could take over if he married this man's sister. So Uncle said yes, and then he married Auntie and took over the flower farm."

Tak-Tak pulled on Frank's shirt. Frank looked at him. "My sister talks a lot sometimes," he said.

Frank smiled. "Yes, she does." He turned to Sumiko. "I wouldn't mind meeting your cousin who's working on the irrigation. My brothers want to farm someday. Some of the reservation is irrigated, but our land isn't yet."

Sumiko didn't reply. She didn't know if she was allowed to talk to an Indian. Maybe her cousins would be mad at her. Ichiro had such a bad temper, maybe he would throw something against the wall if he found out.

"You're not supposed to be on camp, are you?" she asked.

"I came with my uncle. He delivers supplies."

"Do you have an icebox?" said Tak-Tak suddenly.

Frank blew another bubble and popped it. "Yes, but there's no ice in it at the moment."

"How come?" said Tak-Tak.

Frank ignored him and stretched his back.

"Are you poor?" said Tak-Tak.

"Takao!" said Sumiko. "That's rude!"

But instead of turning on Tak-Tak, Frank snapped at Sumiko. "They take our land and put *you* on it. They give you electricity. They give you ice. I found a sandwich one of you threw on the road." He glared at her.

Sumiko felt anger rise in herself. "We didn't ask to be here. It wasn't my sandwich!"

Frank's eyes cooled off a bit. But he pushed through the bean plants, and Sumiko watched him run off.

"He liked me," said Tak-Tak. "But not you. Doesn't he have electricity?"

"I don't know. Maybe not." Sumiko watched as Frank disappeared in the distance. Her family was poor, but they had electricity. "He must have electricity," she finally declared. "We have it, and we're practically in jail."

18

BACK AT THE BARRACK THAT EVENING AS SUMIKO lounged around inside, Mr. Moto called out to her. "I have an announcement, Sumiko!"

She rushed out—anything was more exciting than lying around the barrack fending off the ultimate boredom. He stood by his plot of land holding a handful of droopy bean cuttings as if he were holding gold.

"Shouldn't those be in water?" she asked.

"That's why I need your help! You know all about farming!"

"You want me to help?" Sumiko's heart actually pounded, kind of like when she had gotten that birthday party invitation.

He handed her half the cuttings. "I'll tell you what. You plant these, and I'll plant the rest, and we'll have a contest to see who can grow the most beans! I'll do the hardest labor, and you provide the expertise. And you can plant all the flowers you have room for." A section of dirt just for herself! Mr. Moto's face lit up as he continued. "A nursery owner from outside camp donated some trees to the camp. I'm going to try to get one of those for our garden."

Mr. Moto had gathered rocks and more hardened wood from the mountains. He planned to use the wood to carve a statue of a samurai. That evening Sumiko drew diagrams planning her section of garden. She drew and drew. Meanwhile, Mr. Moto moved the rocks from here to there and there to here, trying to decide where they looked best. Then Sumiko threw away the diagrams and decided just to plant a profusion of flowers. She lugged bucket after bucket of water from the latrine to make it easier for Mr. Moto to dig into the hard ground.

As they worked, though, something started to bother her. Maybe she should politely tell him that the desert sun might kill their cuttings. But he must know that. Anybody would know a thing like that! Wouldn't they? She didn't want to embarrass him by telling him something he should have known already. But the more she didn't speak, the more she wanted to speak. Finally she told Mr. Moto, "It'll be too sunny for the plants! We need to cover them with cheesecloth."

Mr. Moto looked up in surprise. "Nobody else is using cheesecloth." He quickly added, "I just mention that for conversation. You're probably right."

Sumiko ignored the part about nobody else using cheesecloth. "I could make you a cover. Maybe Auntie will let me order cheesecloth from Sears." Everybody in camp ordered from Sears; the deliveries were a great excitement. She stepped forward so Auntie wouldn't hear. "In the meantime, I could use a piece of my sheet. My sheet's too long for the cot anyway."

"I'll tell you what. I'll buy your cheesecloth." It always amazed Sumiko that no matter how poor grown-ups were, they all seemed to have enough money for gum or cheesecloth or whatever else a kid might want.

"We'll have to use some sheet in the meanwhile," she said. "I'm going to plant stock, and they usually like to germinate in cooler conditions."

"Of course, stock—those are . . ."

"They're beautiful flowers!"

Sumiko hurried into her home and pounced on her sheet, ripping a section off with her teeth. Auntie would kill her if she ever found out. Mr. Moto hid the sheet in his house—what a wonderful man he was!—while Sumiko brought Tak-Tak to the big pile of scrap wood that had been left over from building the camp.

The pile was where everybody got wood for building tables and chairs. Sumiko and Tak-Tak searched for wood to use for stakes to hold up the sheet.

Tak-Tak seemed happy as he searched the pile. She felt strangely happy too, though she couldn't imagine why climbing around in the moonlight on a pile of wood should make her happy.

Finally they found ten stakes, more than they needed for the moment. But eventually, if she got her cheesecloth from Sears, she'd need all ten. Night had fallen. The air was cool, and Sumiko was happy. The ultimate boredom seemed far, far away.

The next day when Auntie had gone to her sewing club, Sumiko erected a cover for the seeds and cuttings. The sun seemed to be frying the top of her head, but she felt she needed to get the cover up as quickly as possible. When she finished, she stepped back and admired her work.

Tak-Tak called from the barrack. "Are you finished?"

"Yes!"

"I think we should take ice to the Indian boy," he said.

She turned her attention away from the garden. "He doesn't live in the bean field."

"Maybe he's there. Please?"

Sumiko thought it over. "I don't even like that boy," she said. But Tak-Tak's face fell, and she was in a good mood. And *she* certainly deserved some ice. "All right, let's go, then."

They got ice and walked to their tunnel in the bean field. Tak-Tak quickly ate his ice, but Sumiko ate hers slowly, so she'd have some left in case the rude boy showed up. But finally all her ice had melted, and she drank down the cool water.

19

ONCE, IN THIRD GRADE, SUMIKO'S TEACHER HAD ASKED everybody in class to write a paragraph about their favorite thing. She had titled her paper "Dirt." Some of the other girls had made fun of her for that, and when she read her paper, they giggled and laughed at her. The other girls liked dancing and music and dolls. One girl even liked cars. But not dirt. Sumiko loved dolls, but she loved dirt more.

Sumiko *still* loved dirt. It smelled really good. The problem with the dirt in Poston was that it didn't smell good to her. In fact, it hardly smelled at all. So one morning when Bull was getting ready to leave for work, Sumiko sat up.

"Bull?"

"Awake already?" he said.

"Mr. Moto let me plant some seeds in the garden out front. They were Uncle's special stock seeds. But I'm worried because they haven't sprouted yet. The dirt doesn't smell right."

"You need organic matter."

"You mean like Baba's manure? Where will I get it?"

He leaned over, pinched her nose, and said, "Everywhere. It doesn't have to be *Baba's* manure." He rushed out the door, leaving her pondering the word *everywhere*.

Later she got some old cans from the mess hall kitchen and looked around. Sachi and some other kids passed by. "What are you doing?" Sachi asked.

"Gathering organic matter."

The kids all just gave her a funny look and walked on. Maybe she would never fit in with most kids! But the funny thing was, she didn't care, because she was too excited.

First she gathered some leaves from the surrounding area. She crumpled up the leaves. Then she went to the Camp Three chicken coop and used a piece of wood to scoop chicken droppings into a can. Then she mixed the droppings with the leaves and some dirt. Then she mixed it all into the soil in the garden.

When the sun got too hot to continue working,

she went inside and lay down and thought about how healthy she was making the dirt.

Every morning, if she'd slept inside, she would open her eyes and run outside to check her seeds. If she'd slept outside, she would just jump off her cot and be right there at her garden. But inside or out, every day she saw the same thing: nothing. She didn't think Uncle's Sumiko Strain could possibly be a failure, so she must have done something wrong. She was surprised at how bitter that made her feel. It made her feel useless. Even some of the beans hardly seemed to be growing.

One morning when Bull had already left, she stopped Ichiro just as he was rushing off for work. "Ich!"

"I'm late, Sumiko, what is it?"

"I planted some flower seeds, and they haven't bloomed yet. They were a new strain of stock that Uncle was developing in the shed."

"Sumiko, you know it's too hot now for stock to germinate. They need colder weather."

"But these are special seeds!"

He just shook his head and hurried off.

Later she tried digging up a seed and saw that it hadn't changed a bit since she'd planted it a couple of weeks ago. Maybe she had lost the knack for farming since she'd been in camp. She dug up another seed, and her jaw dropped as she saw the tiny white beginnings of a sprout.

"It's growing!" she cried out. She looked around;

she was alone. It was growing! She gently covered up both seeds again.

She made sure to sleep outside that night, and when she woke up the next morning, she fell immediately upon the garden. Three gorgeous tendrils of green poked out from the dirt. She felt a wave of paranoia and looked around. What if a bug ate some of her sprouts? Maybe sprouts like this were a treasure trove to a desert bug! So she spent the next hour constructing a tiny dome out of a piece of sheet. She would lay the dome over the seedlings in case any bugs struck in the night.

Every evening she would place a tiny dome she made over each of her new sprouts. This took a long time. Once, just before sunset, she heard Bull and Ichiro talking behind her. She could tell they wanted her to hear.

"What do you think, Bull, is she losing her mind?"

"Could be, could be. The sun may have gone to her head."

"Yep, I hear that happens sometimes."

She just ignored them.

As the weeks passed the gardens and fields of Poston grew more and more lush. Sumiko was shocked when her flowers bloomed. She'd expected them to be peach, but instead they were the colors of the rainbow. And there was plenty of organic matter for everyone. Camps One, Two, and Three each had started a poultry farm and a hog farm. The plan was to make the whole camp self-sustaining as quickly as possible. Supposedly, the people of Poston weren't in jail; they were doing their patriotic duty, supporting the war by staying in this camp. Anyway, that's what some people said. Of course, Ichiro thought some of the people were *inu*.

Sumiko's flowers quickly grew so profuse that Sumiko thought she and Mr. Moto ought to enter their garden in the Camp Three gardening competition. He didn't want to. "We won't win," he insisted. He was riled because he hadn't gotten any of the free trees from the nursery. "Did you see the Kadokawa garden? They got two trees."

Still, Sumiko thought their garden was getting more beautiful every day. The flower stalks grew two and a half feet high, and every morning the flowers filled the air near the barrack with the scent of cloves. It was like a flower forest.

And the flowers were bigger than the ones they used to grow on the farm. The purple ones looked like grapes growing from trees. Each time Sumiko saw her garden, she thought of Uncle and how much he had loved to work in his shed. She wrote to Jiichan and Uncle telling them about her garden.

Dear Jiichan,

I am growing a new garden using Uncle's special stock seeds I got from his shed. The seeds are called Sumiko Strain. They are growing very well. The garden is very beautiful.

I am staying busy, as you would want me to do. I am writing on a blank sheet of paper!

Love,
Sumiko

Jiichan, being Jiichan, wrote back and didn't even mention the garden or the blank paper. In fact, his whole letter was about food. He just talked about all the foods he used to eat in their old life and how much he missed all that.

Every morning before the day grew too hot, Sumiko checked for weeds and bugs in her garden. And once a week she went to the chicken coop and filled a can with chicken droppings. Tak-Tak, naturally, liked to help her with that chore. Nobody else could smell the dirt beneath the scent of the flowers, but Sumiko could smell it. It smelled good.

The camp paper still carried story after story about the loss of discipline among the children, and Sumiko knew the grown-ups talked about that a lot. But when the adults talked about her, they just joked, "All Sumiko cares about is dirt."

20

THE CRAZIEST THING HAPPENED IN SEPTEMBER. THE *Poston Chronicle* reported that now that the government had gotten them all in here, it was trying to get them all out. There was a severe labor shortage in America, and even *Nikkei* were in demand as workers, especially for picking crops. As long as *Nikkei* didn't work on the coast, and as long as their off-camp jobs were approved, they could resettle outside camp.

None of the people Sumiko or her family knew took the idea of leaving seriously. First of all, even families who had lost thousands of dollars were being offered a resettlement fee of just one hundred dollars from the government to set up their new homes.

Ichiro and Bull scoffed at the idea of leaving. Ichiro was especially furious. "I lose everything I've worked for, my father and grandfather are arrested, and they want me to pick crops to help a white man make money?"

"It would be like being on parole," agreed Bull.

Auntie didn't want the family to leave either. She worried about Sumiko and Tak-Tak. "Would they be safe outside camp?" she asked anxiously. "The ladies in my sewing group say a Japanese got shot at in the Midwest."

Sumiko agreed with Ichiro. They hadn't owned their farm, but those flowers were *theirs*. Those flowers might as well have been set on fire by the government. And she liked how in camp she was treated as an equal, even if she didn't fit in. Nobody had held a birthday party yet, but she knew if they did, she would be invited just like everybody else.

A few people who'd already left camp to pick crops had already written back to say that conditions were difficult and even dangerous for *Nikkei* outside of camp. And the new rules about resettlement didn't include people like Uncle and Jiichan who were imprisoned by the Department of Justice.

"Look," said Ichiro, "if we go out, we'll have to cower to *hakujin* night and day. We won't be able to walk down the street holding our heads high."

Personally, Sumiko didn't want to leave camp and

go someplace completely unknown where someone might shoot at her and Tak-Tak. Tak-Tak was safest right here. Sumiko had even started to think she could open a little flower store right here in Poston.

While she and Mr. Moto picked at weeds in the garden later, he told her his nephews were leaving camp to work on a farm picking crops. "They used to own their own farm," he said. "I wish they would stay here." He looked thoughtful. "But I wish my son would leave. All he does is gamble or lie in bed."

"Are *you* thinking about leaving?" Sumiko asked.

"I'm too old to start over under those circumstances," he said. "I'll wait until they let us out with all our civil rights." Sumiko wasn't even sure what *civil rights* were, but the grown-ups talked about them all the time. Mr. Moto looked very sad then, and Sumiko figured he was thinking about his civil rights. Instead, he said, "Did you notice a few of my bean plants died?"

"Yes, but don't worry. Every so often you lose a plant. That's part of farming."

Mr. Moto actually looked as if he were about to cry. "I lost seven. Maybe I'm not meant to be a farmer."

He hung his head low and trudged into his barrack. What an emotional man! Sumiko felt responsible somehow, felt she'd let him down. After all, there was a man on the next block whose bean plants were thriving. She had seen Mr. Moto eye the man's garden competitively, even jealously. So she prepared all of Mr. Moto's area with extra organic matter and took a can of water to gather more cuttings for him at the bean tunnels.

She also brought two cups of ice. In case that Frank boy was there, it would be rude to bring just one cup.

She knew Frank was there before she saw him. He wasn't even hiding, just examining the beans. "You're not supposed to be here," she called out.

He glanced mildly at her, as if she were a fly and he were considering swatting her. "This is *our* land."

"It's ours for now. Anyway, you weren't using it."

"What is it with you? You think you have to be using land for it to be worth something?"

She decided right then not to offer him any ice. She felt satisfied when he couldn't help but glance at the two cups. "What are you doing here?" she said.

"Just seeing what you people are doing. What are *you* doing here?" He glanced again at the cups of ice.

"I hope you don't think I brought this for you," she said.

They glared at each other. Then he tilted his head the way he had done the first time she saw him. He smiled and took a cup from her. "You're a bad liar," he said.

"Well, at least you could say thank you."

He said it with a mouth full of ice. They saw some

white men walking toward the field, so they slipped into a bean tunnel. They sucked on their ice as the men approached and walked by. Sumiko thought of whites as people you had to be quiet around, and Frank seemed to feel the same way.

Sumiko and Frank didn't talk, just greedily ate their ice and then drank the cool water from the ice that had melted. When they finished, Frank looked surprised, as if he'd forgotten she was even there. "So they're keeping you here until the end of the war?" he said.

"I don't know. It's kind of confusing. Now the government wants us to leave. They want us working outside to support the war effort. One family who left camp wrote back to their relatives and said they had to drive ten miles to find a grocery store that would serve them."

"The Office of Indian Affairs wants you to stay," he said.

"I thought the Indians didn't want us here," Sumiko said, surprised.

"Some of them don't." Frank looked at her with that steady gaze of his.

"I thought *you* didn't want us here."

"I didn't. Neither did my family." Then he did that thing again where he tilted his head a touch. "But we've changed our minds. The government is spending money to bring water to the reservation. You're cultivating the land."

"That's because we're slave labor."

"I just mean you're here anyway." He lay back. "It's nice in this field." He turned lazily to her. "So what kind of flowers did your family raise?"

"We specialized in *kusabana*. That means 'weed-flower.'" She felt pride well up in her. "We had some of the best *kusabana* at the market. We also grew carnations."

"Where were you born?"

"California." She waited for him to reply. When he didn't, she said, "What about you? What kind of Indian are you?"

"Mohave. We were here first. Then came the Chemehuevi. Now the government wants to bring Hopi and Navajo onto the reservation. In fact, they're going to take over your barracks when the war ends."

"Why would they want to do that?"

"It's better conditions than some of them have now," he explained. "So what happened to your farm?"

"It's gone."

"Gone where?"

"I mean gone for us. A lot of people lost everything they had during the evacuation." She hugged her knees to her chest.

He shrugged. "You're not the first people to lose things."

Sumiko stared at him, then shocked herself by bursting into tears. Frank sat up, looking really surprised. Then all of a sudden she pictured Baba's big eyes, and she cried about *that*. Then she was thinking about her grandfather and uncle shivering up in North Dakota, and she cried about *that*.

Frank let her cry for a while and then said nervously, "Don't go crazy on me here."

But she kept crying.

Finally he sat up and touched her arm. "Weedflower Girl," he said, "don't cry." He spoke with such concern, it was as if he were a different boy. Seeing this different boy made her stop crying. Then someone called his name, and he became nonchalant again. "I better go. I'll be back in two days. Bring me more ice." He pushed his way out of the vines.

She scrambled after him, calling out, "My name is Sumiko, not 'Weedflower Girl.'"

21

SUMIKO WISHED THERE WERE A LIBRARY IN CAMP SO SHE could look up *Mohave*. There *was* a library, actually, but it had about seven books so far. There weren't any teachers to ask either. She wasn't sure whether she would ever have to go to school again. In October everybody still talked of building a schoolhouse, but even if someone built a schoolhouse, there would be no books, no desks and chairs, and no teachers. When and if the time came, everyone said the kids would just have to drag their chairs to school.

Sumiko kept busy gardening. It was selfish, but when someone asked for some of her flowers, she said no. Ordinarily, she would have given people all the flowers they wanted, but she had secretly entered the garden in the camp contest and didn't want to sacrifice even one blossom. She had felt like a spy filling out the entry form.

Besides gardening, Sumiko's main pastime became trying to stay cool. Some people became obsessed with shade. Mr. Moto and a couple of men on Sumiko's block would take their chairs outside, set them in the shade, and then move the chairs around as the shade moved. Mr. Moto called them "shadeseekers," as opposed to another group of men on the block who were called "windchasers." They sought out not only shade but breezes as well.

Sumiko still couldn't get used to the heat. It made her head feel foggy. She dreaded the afternoons and the inescapable heat. She tried both windchasing and shadeseeking. In the end, however, her solution was to try to stay as still as possible during the hottest hours of the day. The problem was that when she stayed still, all sorts of thoughts pushed their way into her head. She thought about how scary it would be to leave camp, and she thought about Frank. She wondered if he qualified as a "friend." Sachi was a friend, and if Frank was a friend as well, that meant she had two friends. Three, counting Mr. Moto.

Friendship was really different from the way she had envisioned it all these years. It seemed a lot more complicated. She'd thought friends just hung around together and held the same opinions on just about everything.

Two days after she'd last seen Frank there, Sumiko returned to the same bean tunnel. When she got there, it had been cut down! But Frank called out to her from somewhere else. She saw him stand up, waving from some brush in the distance. She walked over and handed him his ice. He didn't say a word as he slurped at it.

She had also brought a piece of snake Mr. Moto had cooked and salted. When Frank finished the ice, he said, "What is that?"

"I brought you some salted snake to eat."

He reared back a bit. "I can't eat snake!"

"How come? It's good." She was still holding the meat between her fingers. She felt insulted.

Frank spoke patiently, as if to a child. "Mohave believe that some animals may be some of our ancestors come to visit us. So we can't exactly eat them."

"What about cows?"

"That's ridiculous. What ancestor would come back as a cow?"

"Well, I don't know. Maybe a fat ancestor."

"I don't have any fat ancestors."

They sat quietly for a moment. It felt awkward.

"Why aren't you watching your brother?" he asked.

"He's out . . . somewhere."

"Do your parents watch him?"

Sumiko didn't know who was watching him. There were only Japanese around, so who would hurt him? "My parents died in a car crash."

He seemed genuinely disturbed to hear that. "I'm sorry."

"I was just a little girl," she said. She was pleased with how that had come out. It had sounded rather worldly.

"And now you're . . . ?" He seemed amused.

She couldn't tell if he was trying to insult her. "Now I'm a big girl, of course."

"Sensitive," he muttered.

"Well, what about you?" she asked. "What do your parents do?"

"My mother is a tribal secretary." He turned away from her. "My father is gone."

"Gone dead or gone away?"

He looked at the ground. "The first."

"I'm sorry."

He paused. "It's a very bad thing to talk about the dead," he said quietly. Then, even more quietly, he added, "I miss him." He almost whispered, "He had a heart attack." He looked around as if someone might be watching. He'd whispered so quietly, she had to think a moment before she figured out what he'd said. He suddenly pulled gum out of his pocket and unwrapped it. "My brother Joseph was asking about your flower farm," he said, putting the gum in his mouth. He offered her some, but she declined. "One of my brothers joined the army a few months ago, and Joseph is going to leave for basic training soon. But I think I told you that when they come back, they're going to farm. My brother says the water you're bringing in is going to change our lives."

So she told him about disbudding flowers, and about grading, and about the different types of flowers they raised, and about the flower mart, and about everything else she could think of. And also about the ponds and waterfalls men were building in camp.

"You use the irrigated water to build your ponds?"

"No, well water."

He nodded thoughtfully. "We have a well. But in the past Mohave were always dry farmers. There's a little irrigation on the reservation but not much. Did you irrigate your flower farm?"

"Uh-huh, we used ditch irrigation. We didn't even use turnouts. It was very simple."

"What's a turnout?"

"That's the little thingamajig that lets water onto the field from the main ditch."

He looked at her intently, as if memorizing what she said. "Who set up the irrigation?"

"Mostly Bull, but Ichiro and Uncle helped."

"Is Bull at your home now?"

"He's laying concrete today."

Through a gap in the brush, Sumiko saw Sachi and some other kids running and laughing through the fields. A man yelled out to them, "Hey, be careful there. This isn't a playground!"

They didn't listen to the man, just kept running. "Nobody listens anymore," Sumiko said.

"What do you think about Joseph and Bull meeting for a talk? Before Joseph ships out?" Frank said.

"I don't know." She didn't think it was a good idea to tell Bull about Frank. She didn't want to get in trouble for talking to an Indian.

He stood up. "All right. I have to go pick up my baby sister at my mother's friend's house. You think about it, though."

22

On the morning the judges were supposed to look over the gardens, Sumiko still hadn't told Mr. Moto that she'd entered them in the contest.

She was sitting at the table in her barrack getting up the courage to go tell him when someone knocked at the door. "Come in!" she called out.

It was Mr. Moto. "I thought you might want to come outside," he said.

She walked slowly to the door, then stopped and blurted out, "I entered us in the contest!"

She thought he might be angry, but instead he laughed. "Well, I entered us also!"

They took down the cheesecloth so the judges

could get an unfettered view of the garden. Sumiko cleaned up all the spent weedflowers, since there was nothing uglier than a spent weedflower. She got ice water in case the judges were hot. And she and Mr. Moto moved the crickets and snakes away, in case any of the judges didn't like such things. They brought out a few chairs for the judges to sit on under a cheesecloth tent Mr. Moto had erected.

And then they waited. Sumiko didn't tell anyone, but she even wrote out a little speech in case they won first prize and someone asked them to say a few words.

Sumiko looked at the garden. Mr. Moto had built two long ledges on one side and let some kind of vine fall over the ledges. That way their garden looked almost tropical—here in the desert! And Sumiko had gone through her flower forest and cut off a flower here and there, so that the stalks were different heights in some places. She felt this gave the impression that the flowers were wild and not cultivated. And the topper for the whole garden were the long pieces of wood that Mr. Moto had carved into perfect facsimiles of bamboo.

When the judges came around, a number of people from the block stood around to watch. There were seven judges. Some of them knelt down and looked closely at the plants, while others stood far back to get more perspective. They all took notes on pads of paper.

Nobody drank any ice water, and nobody sat under the cheesecloth tent. And nobody asked a single question. After a few minutes the judges smiled stiffly and left.

Mr. Moto and Sumiko looked at each other. "Well, anyway, I think it's a beautiful garden!" he said. Then he hung his head sadly. "Too bad we have no trees." His face grew even sadder. "Sakagami-san has miniature sailboats in his pond." Sumiko felt pretty disappointed and even jealous of Mr. Sakagami.

That day the paper carried an item about an Indian basketball team from the local high school coming to camp after dinner to play against the Camp Three all-star basketball team. The all-stars had never played together before; still, it was a big event. The Indians had played in Camps One and Two before, but this was their first trip to Sumiko's camp. The paper said that the Indians had been told to "stay away from the Camp Three girls."

When Sumiko read the article, she suspected it was written just for her by someone who somehow knew that she knew Frank. She realized her suspicion was ridiculous, but she couldn't stop herself from feeling that way.

The basketball court was dirt that had been sprayed with water to create a hard pack. Everybody in camp was curious to see the Indian team. In the early evening there was a silence when the Indians stepped off their bus. The Indians and the Japanese looked at each other curiously. Sumiko followed in a crowd of kids as the Indians walked to the court. The Indians were taller than most of the Japanese players, except for the Japanese center, a boy who actually had to duck when he entered doorways. But on a good day he was about as fast as a turtle.

Though the Indians and the Japanese seemed curious about each other, Sumiko didn't know if they liked each other. They seemed to want to stay separate. She could tell by how they stood at a distance when they looked at each other.

The Indians all wore their hair short, not long like in pictures Sumiko had seen, and their names were either Anglo or Spanish. Sumiko had thought Frank and his friends might have been unusual, since they all wore their hair short. But so did these older boys.

The Japanese were fast and pesky, and the game stayed close. The crowd cheered wildly for the all-stars. But the Indians won by three points.

After the game a Japanese girl was talking to one of the Indian players when all of a sudden a Japanese boy stepped between them and said warningly, "You stay away from our girls." Sumiko recognized the boy—he lived on the same block as her. She worried what would happen if he found out she knew Frank.

Before the player could reply, the center for the

Indian team came over and said, "He's not interested in *your* girls."

"What's wrong with our girls?" said the Japanese boy. He tried to push the Indian center, but the Japanese center held him back.

Members of both teams had been shaking hands with each other. Now there was a silence like the silence at the party when Sumiko had walked into the living room. It rolled across the crowd in the same way. A moment ago everybody had seemed happy to have played a great game, but now both teams were glaring at each other. Then Bull was there, slapping the boy on the shoulder and saying, "There's nothing wrong with our girls." He reached out to shake hands with the Indian center. "Great game—we'll get you next time!" The center hesitated but nodded, and people started to disperse.

Later Sumiko saw a couple of boys about Tak-Tak's age, following the girl who'd talked to the Indian. The boys were saying, "Indian lover" and pulling at her skirt as she walked with her head high. Ichiro always said that holding your head high was a sign of dignity.

Seeing the boys taunt the girl shook Sumiko up, because she was starting to think Frank wasn't so bad. In fact, she almost liked him. If people pulled at her skirt and called her names, she wondered if she would have the courage to hold her head high like that girl. Whenever she'd thought of having friends, she'd thought about how they would act toward her. Now she saw that if she and Frank were friends, she had responsibilities.

When she got home, she found something hanging on her door: a yellow ribbon. Third place! She grabbed the ribbon and ran into Mr. Moto's barrack, forgetting for the moment about the day's events.

"Congratulations!" he said. He slapped her on the back. "I cooked you up some snake!"

23

After the basketball game Sumiko made extra sure that nobody saw her when she went to the fields. But the next few times she went, Frank wasn't there anyway.

By late October the camp had managed to find enough teachers to start a school, which was to be held in empty barracks. One day Sumiko and Sachi walked by the barracks where some teachers had just moved in. "One of the teachers is Negro," Sachi said. "I saw her. Another one is German. Her father is a Nazi. I saw her, too."

Sumiko never knew what ratio of lies to truth Sachi told, and even if she knew the ratio, she wouldn't have known which was the truth percentage and which was not.

Just to find out how it felt to tell a whopper, Sumiko said, "One of the teachers is from the circus. She used to be a trapeze artist." Sachi looked wonderingly at Sumiko, which made Sumiko feel kind of good. Lying certainly offered satisfactions, but the problem was it left a bad aftertaste.

On the first day of school Sumiko braided her hair and put on her mint green dress. It was tight under the arms and shorter than it used to be. At first she thought it had shrunk, but then she realized she'd grown. But it was still the best dress she owned. She and Tak-Tak each took a chair from their home and stepped outside. As they walked they saw dozens of other kids also carrying their chairs in the dust.

Sumiko dropped Tak-Tak off at his classroom and saw that his teacher *was* Negro. She wondered whether her own teacher would be the daughter of a Nazi!

Inside her classroom there were no tables; in fact, there was nothing at all except a young, sweaty white woman standing at the front of the room. She held up a sign that read I AM MISS KELLY. Miss Kelly asked the kids to set their chairs along the walls.

"I am Miss Kelly," said Miss Kelly. "This is my first teaching assignment, and I'm very excited to be here." A drop of sweat fell into her eye, and she wiped it away. Sumiko noticed dust on Miss Kelly's skirt. "I'd like everybody to go around the room and tell us your name and what your parents did before the war."

The kids mostly obeyed glumly, though some of the bad boys slouched in their chairs and openly chewed gum. Miss Kelly seemed nervous. When Sumiko's turn came, she stood up and said, "Sumiko Matsuda. We were flower farmers."

When everyone had finished, Miss Kelly made them sing patriotic songs for an hour. Then Miss Kelly asked whether anybody had any questions.

Someone raised his hand. "Miss Kelly!"

"Yes."

"Why aren't you married?"

Everyone giggled. Miss Kelly's mouth fell open, and then she smiled and said, "That's personal."

The boy raised his hand again, but she ignored him. Nobody else raised a hand. For a second Miss Kelly looked like she might cry. Sumiko felt sorry for her.

A boy called out, "Will you marry me?" Everybody laughed. Then Miss Kelly passed around a novel called *The King of the Island*. It was an old beat-up book that nobody had ever heard of. Miss Kelly said each teacher had been given exactly one book for class. Miss Kelly made everybody in class read a page out loud and then pass it on to the next person.

After that it was lunchtime, and after lunch Miss Kelly let them leave early, partly because it was the first day and partly because none of the boys had returned from lunch.

In Camp Three there were Caucasian teachers, *Nisei* teachers, and one Negro teacher. *Nisei* were the second generation of *Nikkei*, but the first generation born in America. For most of the *Nisei* teachers, this was their first teaching job. Though they'd graduated college with teaching degrees, before camp they hadn't been able to find jobs because of their race.

At one time Sumiko had been looking forward to school, but now that she had her garden, school seemed kind of useless. The only people who seemed to take it seriously were the teachers.

One of the Caucasian teachers didn't last long. Turnover was high from the start, but this woman suffered an actual nervous breakdown and had to leave. Sumiko thought maybe it was the dust that drove teachers away. You couldn't escape it. Sometimes you could ignore it, but when you had nothing to do, you were aware of dirt grains on your scalp and up your nose and in your eyes, and no matter if you closed your door, you found it all over your sheets and your floors. Some of the Christians in camp said God was testing them with this dust. Tak-Tak said, "What happens if you fail the dust test?" Sumiko didn't know.

Though she knew it was wrong, Sumiko couldn't help feeling kind of satisfied when the teachers left.

White people had put them in this camp, and yet they couldn't take it. She remembered how a few months ago one of the planes that buzzed camp just to harass them had crashed. And several *Nikkei* had applauded. "It serves them right!" people had said.

Sumiko figured that *hakujin* thought they were better than the Japanese and the Indians; the Indians didn't seem to particularly like whites *or* Japanese; and Japanese didn't want to socialize with the Indians and resented the whites. So nobody liked anybody much. She told this to Ichiro, and he said, "That's why we have laws." She told this to Bull, and he said, "Well, remember the Quakers." Sumiko had forgotten all about them and about the woman who'd taken care of Mrs. Ono's dog, and she had even forgotten about Miss Kelly, who was nice enough to work here teaching them when she could have gotten a job outside instead.

Ichiro and his friends liked to argue about laws, race, and camp. One night a friend of Ichiro's who was visiting exclaimed that he was sick of camp and was going to look into finding work outside. He was one of Ichiro's most outspoken friends. Before Pearl Harbor they used to double-date in their fancy clothes.

"Camp is jail," he told them. He and Ichiro were leaning against a wall smoking. Sumiko watched the smoke wind through the dim barrack.

"We were put here to be safe," Auntie said.

"Mother, that is not why they put us in here," Ichiro said.

Ichiro's friend muttered, "Your mother talks like an *inu*." Sumiko stayed very still so nobody would notice her and make her leave.

Ichiro said, "My mother is not an *inu*. She just doesn't understand."

Auntie said, "I understand all I need to."

Then everybody started yelling about exactly why they were in camp. Tak-Tak ran to his bed and pulled the covers over his head.

"We're in camp because of prejudice, pure and simple," shouted Ichiro's friend.

"We were put here for our own protection," Auntie insisted again. "To protect us from all the people who hate us."

Ichiro said, "That's ridiculous. If I hate someone, should the person I hate be put in jail to protect him? And now there are rumors that they're going to start drafting us right out of this jail."

Bull was sitting at the table reading the day's *Chronicle* and acting as if he couldn't hear a thing.

But for some reason Ichiro turned on him. "Are you going to be willing to fight if your family has no rights?"

Sumiko was shocked. She knew that because of their ancestry, *Nisei* had been declared ineligible to join the military. And she'd heard that some *Nisei* were trying to get the government to make them eligible again. But she had assumed it would never happen. Yet Ichiro seemed to feel it *would* happen.

"I'm going to be willing to fight *because* my family has no rights," Bull said.

"Can't you see that's wrong?" Ichiro shouted.

"Then let's show them how wrong they are," Bull said quietly.

"It's their responsibility to learn to live by their own laws. Why do we have to teach them to follow their own laws?"

Sumiko waited for Bull to answer. But Bull didn't answer; Sumiko knew there was no answer. Ichiro and Bull glared at each other.

"Nobody's going to want to serve with us," Ichiro finally said. "Nobody's going to want to command us. Nobody wants us, Bull."

Tak-Tak sat up and said, "Bull?"

Bull whipped toward him. "Can't you stupid kids—" He stopped. Tak-Tak looked mortified.

Sumiko pulled Tak-Tak out of bed and took him outside to look at Mr. Moto's snake, which was sleeping. Mr. Moto had kept this particular snake for a while and seemed to have grown fond of it. It was unusually long, and it even seemed a little fat. People on the block called it Snakie, as if it was a pet.

She put her arms around Tak-Tak as they studied

the snake. "Will you come to watch if I ever play in a marbles tournament?" he asked her.

"Yes, if you want."

"Okay," he said. "Snakie's sleeping."

"His eyes are open."

"Mr. Moto says they sleep with their eyes open," Tak-Tak said, clearly proud he knew something Sumiko didn't.

"Really? You're so smart!"

He beamed.

"I like Snakie," Tak-Tak said. "We could set him free before anyone eats him."

Sumiko considered the idea. But setting Snakie free would be like stealing him from Mr. Moto. She figured a lot of the kids stole things. But you couldn't steal from a neighbor; you had to draw the line somewhere. She rested her chin on Tak-Tak's head and said, "Don't do anything with Mr. Moto's snake. It belongs to him."

She gazed out at the dark forms of mesquite trees in the distance. Ichiro said the administration had decided Poston needed a barbed-wire fence, allegedly to keep the cattle owned by the Indians from wandering into camp. Indians were going to put up the fence. Since nobody had ever seen one of these cattle wandering into camp, that reasoning wasn't going over very well, especially with people like Ichiro and his friends.

Tak-Tak said, "Is Bull mad at me?"

"Of course not."

Tak-Tak looked surprised. "He said 'stupid.'"

"He didn't mean it."

Sumiko could smell cigarette smoke from inside. She could hear that the grown-ups seemed to have finished arguing. "Are you ready for bed?" she asked.

"Can I say good night to Snakie?"

"Okay."

Tak-Tak leaned forward until his glasses clinked against the cage. "Good night, Snakie." Snakie didn't react; his eyes just stared out into the night. "He's sleeping," Tak-Tak said again.

Sumiko led him back inside. Ichiro went off with his friend as the rest of the family got ready for bed.

When it was dark, Bull got out of bed and knelt by Tak-Tak's bed. "Tak-chan," he said, "I want to tell you something."

"What?"

"I want to tell you a knock-knock joke."

Tak-Tak started laughing even before Bull told the joke.

"Knock, knock."

"Who's there?"

"Mesquite."

"Mesquite who? Whisper it! Whisper it!" He was giggling hard now.

Bull leaned over and whispered something into the ear of Tak-Tak, who erupted into utter hysterics. What a nice sound that was!

When he calmed down, Bull stroked Tak-Tak's forehead and said quietly, "Good night, Tak-chan."

24

DECEMBER WAS THE COLDEST MONTH OF THE YEAR IN THE desert. At first Sumiko had been thrilled at the cooling weather. But when the temperatures hit the thirties at night and nobody owned heaters, she sometimes lay in bed trying to convince herself that she didn't have to go to the latrine. If she moved, cool air would slip in under the blankets. But her need to pee always won out, and she would rush to the latrine wrapped in a blanket. Still, the cold wasn't as bad as the heat, because at least you could escape it. There was no escape at all from heat. After one frigid night Sumiko woke up to discover that Ichiro and Bull had given up their blankets to Sumiko and Tak-Tak. That made her feel safe—and guilty.

The pile of scrap wood quickly grew smaller as people used the wood for bonfires. One day toward the end of December a group of Indians began erecting the barbed-wire fence around camp. *Nikkei* stood around the bonfires watching the fence go up. There was quiet talk against the Indians, complaints like, "Why must we be fenced in instead of their cows?" The fence depressed everybody. Sumiko felt angry seeing the barbed wire stretching past her home. Mr. Moto said the fence ruined the ambience of the garden. Miss Kelly told Sumiko that *ambience* meant "atmosphere." Mr. Moto told her that *atmosphere* meant "the air in outer space." The camp dictionary was missing. Anyway, the fence ruined everything.

Not long before Christmas, Sumiko received a letter from Jiichan.

Dear Sumiko,

I decide to take up poetry. You speak good English. Correct poem and send back to me. I open to criticism.

Christmas happy day
But cold freeze my way
Shikata ga nai
Too much cloud in sky

Please write back quickly with correction. I think my talent is very good, but let me know what you think.

Love,
Jiichan

The letter made Sumiko feel even worse than the fence did. The *Chronicle* was trying to drum up spirit for the Christmas season. Some churches from outside had donated presents for the thousands of children of Poston. But for the second year in a row Sumiko wasn't that interested in the holidays. A story in the paper said that all the blocks would be holding individual parties. But who cared? Christmas seemed like a family event, but Sumiko didn't really feel they were like a family anymore—not exactly. Eating and working together used to keep them close. But in the camp she sometimes hardly even talked to Bull, Ichiro, or Auntie all day.

When Christmas arrived, Mr. Moto roasted snake for everyone in the barrack. Snakie watched benignly from his cage as his fellow snakes went up in smoke.

Mr. Moto wore paper tinsel in his hair all day—there was no real tinsel available because tinfoil was needed for the war effort. Mr. Moto put the snake pieces on a tray, and people used sticks to stab the meat.

Sumiko felt lonely. She could have had a lot of friends, but the other kids who lived nearby just wanted to play poker and steal things. Sachi was so expert at stealing from the canteen that other kids actually paid her to steal for them. Mr. Moto told Sumiko that stealing was "endemic" among the children. Miss Kelly said *endemic* meant "everywhere."

Since Mr. Moto was a widower, Sumiko cleaned up his room for him as a Christmas gift. His son lay on his cot ignoring her. He was handsome but never went out anymore. She felt bad seeing him lying around like that. He was probably afflicted by the ultimate boredom.

"Do you want me to get you some water or ice or anything?"

He looked at her as if from a stupor. "Nuh."

Seeing Mr. Moto's son always made Sumiko dejected.

A couple of months ago he had stolen and lost the money his father had gotten from selling his property. Gambling was an ongoing problem at the camp. A couple of young *Nisei* men had lost the entire remaining savings of their families. Now Mr. Moto's son was supposed to just stay home all the time. Mr. Moto didn't care if his son worked or had friends; he only wanted him to stop gambling. Mr. Moto said that for the young men, there was no meaning in camp life. You couldn't earn much money, you couldn't create a future, you couldn't join the army, you couldn't do anything at all that was meaningful. Mr. Moto said, "What can you do when everything you want is out of reach? You become lazy."

Sumiko put on her increasingly frayed mint green dress and walked with Tak-Tak and Auntie to the party.

The smaller children from her block were already milling about the presents, picking them up and shaking them excitedly. A donated tree rose in the center. The tree was laden with paper ornaments. Tags on the gifts read either BOY or GIRL.

In a corner stood a group of boys who often stole items from the canteen. That very day the *Poston Chronicle* had run a story stating that "severe action" would be taken for anyone caught stealing at the canteen. Sumiko didn't know what kind of severe action could result from stealing a candy bar or hairpins. They were all incarcerated anyway! What more could happen?

She took Tak-Tak's hand. "Come on, I'll open your present with you."

"Okay."

"If you could get anything you wanted, what would it be?" she said.

"Baba."

"Oh!" Sumiko said. She thought he'd forgotten Baba. He hardly ever mentioned her. It made her wish they'd gotten him a horse statue for Christmas.

He opened one of the boys' presents, a wooden car with moving wheels. Tak-Tak smiled almost shyly. "Is it mine?"

"Yes. Do you like it?"

"Yes." He rolled it back and forth a few times. "It's my favorite thing," he said. He spoke with true satisfaction.

For a family present they'd mail-ordered him a stuffed cricket. He'd carried it around all day and placed it carefully on his pillow before they left for the party. They'd considered getting him marbles, but he'd never entered any of the tournaments and, in truth, the other boys were right when they said he wasn't very good at marbles.

Sumiko had received a small lacquered mirror from her family. She'd looked in it in the sun and been kind of surprised at her appearance. Her family hadn't brought a mirror because none of them cared what they looked like except Ichiro, who owned a private mirror. When Sumiko saw herself, she decided it was definitely time to start curling her hair like the older girls. But her skin gleamed and her lips were red, and overall she had to admit she was pleased. In fact, everybody started making fun of her because she'd smiled at herself in the mirror. They said she was conceited, which was one of the worst things a young lady could be.

Tak-Tak played and played with his car. Sumiko sat with him on the floor while everybody else started dancing.

After a while Auntie took Tak-Tak home to sleep.

Sumiko opened one of the girls' presents. It was a cute blond baby doll. She gave it to one of the younger girls. Then someone gave a speech about how great it was to be an American. A few people from the block sang songs.

Sumiko stood around with some kids her age. One boy said, "Let's steal a chicken!" His name was Joji, and he was one of the leaders of the troublemakers.

"What're we gonna do with a chicken?" said another boy.

"Eat it," Joji said.

"But we had chicken for dinner!"

"I'm still hungry."

"But there's food on the table over there."

"Look, do you want to come or not?" Joji demanded.

"All right, all right."

As someone gave another speech Sumiko and Sachi slipped out with the boys. The evening was cool and humid. Sumiko hesitated as the kids ran off. Tonight felt different than usual. It was Christmas; they were locked up probably for the duration of the war; she had lost her dream of a flower shop; she didn't feel like listening to speeches about being an American; and why *shouldn't* she go with them to steal a chicken? She ran after them.

The cool air gusted against her face as she chased after the boys. Sachi gleefully smiled at her as they all raced across camp. Here and there Sumiko heard the music and laughter of the other block parties.

When they reached the chicken coop, they walked in, and Sumiko saw dozens of chickens fast asleep. "Grab the neck!" Joji said. "If you grab their neck at night, they don't squawk."

Another boy grabbed a chicken around the neck, and they all ran like crazy straight out of camp through an area that hadn't been fenced off. Sachi giggled hysterically as they ran. Sumiko hesitated at one point but then caught up. They walked quietly, the lights from the camp growing smaller behind them. "Let's go to the river," someone said.

Sumiko had never been off camp this late. It was kind of thrilling. When they reached the river, she could still see the lights from camp. The boy with the chicken set it down. The chicken shook herself off and clucked a bit.

"Anyone bring matches?" said Joji. Sumiko had once heard that before camp he had been a Goody Two-shoes, straight-A student.

Everybody shook their heads no. "I'm thirsty," said one boy.

"We'll drink chicken blood!" Joji said, but nobody seemed to like that idea.

One of the boys was in the Camp Three Boy Scouts, so he got assigned the task of starting a fire from scratch. They made a pile of the driest sticks they could find and left him to his chore. The chicken just wandered around clucking. She walked right up to Sumiko and clucked and clucked. Sumiko reached down and petted her. The chicken seemed to like that.

They waited and waited for the Boy Scout to start a fire. "I'm getting blisters," he finally said.

"Hurry up before it starts raining!" commanded Joji.

"Well, who's going to kill it even if I start a fire?"

"I will," Joji said. He stood up and grabbed the chicken. Sumiko had just managed to close her eyes when she heard the crack of the hen's neck.

"Hey," said a boy, "I've got matches after all!"

He started the fire while the rest of them tried to pluck the chicken. Joji looked at Sumiko. "Come on, Sumiko, help us. It's a woman's job. Weren't you from a farm?"

"It was a flower farm."

"A farm girl is a farm girl."

Sumiko had never plucked a chicken before. She and Sachi plucked it but didn't do a very good job. It was hard to believe how many feathers the darn thing had. The little downiest feathers were nearly impossible to pull out. She seemed to vaguely remember something about boiling a chicken briefly before you plucked it. But that didn't matter since they didn't have a pot to boil it in. The boys tried to make a spit, but the chicken kept falling into the fire. Finally it started to rain, and they decided it was too late to eat the chicken. They dug a hole with their hands and buried it. Sumiko and Sachi started to cry over the poor chicken. Even one of the younger boys started to cry.

Joji stamped on the dirt over the chicken, then said to Sumiko, "Say a few words."

"About the chicken?" she asked.

"Yeah, you're the one she liked the best."

Sumiko knelt near the burial site. "Um. Dear . . . chicken. We're sorry. We didn't mean to kill you. Well, we did mean to kill you, actually. Um. We're sorry we didn't eat you because now your life was wasted."

"Her life wasn't wasted, her death was," the Boy Scout said.

Then everybody started acting like Sumiko had a special line of communication to the chicken. "Tell it next time we steal a chicken, we'll do it right." "Tell it we're sorry if we hurt it." "Tell it we hope it goes to heaven."

After that the kids told a few ghost stories while Sumiko lay on her back and let rain fall on her face. It felt nice to be outside the camp. She tried to imagine her farm but couldn't picture it for some reason. Those days seemed far, far away.

Eventually, the kids trudged back to camp. As they got closer Sumiko could see that all but the essential lights were out—just a few dim lights illuminating the desert. It must have been late. Rain washed all over them. As they walked one of the boys started singing. He had a beautiful voice, as good as someone in the movies. When he sang "Silent Night," the whole universe seemed silent, except for that amazing voice.

25

SUMIKO KEPT HER GARDEN UP OVER THE WINTER, MAKING sure there were always at least a few blooms. But the fence really did destroy the ambience. One late January day when Sumiko and Tak-Tak were playing *hanafuda* off camp behind some brush near some fields, Frank showed up. She hadn't seen him for a while, and she immediately had two thoughts:

1. She was glad to see him.
2. She was mad because he was was Indian and the Indians had put up a fence.

Even though it was cool out, Tak-Tak immediately cried out, "We forgot to bring you ice!"

Frank smiled and sat down to look over the *hanafuda* cards. "You like cards a lot?"

"Yes. I like marbles, too, but I'm not very good at it. And once I went fishing with my cousins. I liked that, too. I caught one fish."

Sumiko noticed that Frank often glanced at her even when talking to Tak-Tak. She pretended to ignore Frank and concentrate on her cards. Then he stopped glancing at her and started ignoring *her*, so she said, "I don't like the fence the Indians put up." She braced for an argument.

"I don't like it either," he said, and there went her argument.

She tried again. "Nobody has ever tried to escape."

Frank changed the subject. "Did you ask your cousin about meeting my brother?"

Tak-Tak asked, "Bull or Ichiro?"

"Bull," said Sumiko. "No."

"How come?"

"I don't know. It didn't come up."

Frank didn't reply. He suddenly looked bored with the subject, or maybe he was bored with Sumiko. Then he asked with irritation, "Why didn't it come up?"

"'Cause."

"Do you have electricity?" Tak-Tak blurted.

"No," said Frank. "No running water, either."

He pretended to reach behind Tak-Tak's head and pull out a piece of gum. "That's mine!" said Tak-Tak.

Frank handed the gum to Tak-Tak but looked at Sumiko the whole time. "I had a dream about you last night. I hardly ever remember my dreams."

"What was it?"

"You were introducing your cousin to my brother. Mohave value our dreams. Sometimes when my grandfather had an important dream, he used to say, 'I see brightly.' That's how I know you're going to ask your cousin."

"Maybe. I had a dream about *you*. I dreamed we were floating down the river in a raft. I dreamed that twice."

She was surprised at how interested he seemed.

"What else did you see?"

"There were waves like in the ocean." He nodded seriously. "What do you think it means?" she asked.

"How would I know?" He squinted at her. "What's that on your lips?"

"It's lipstick I borrowed from my friend Sachi."

"Is that the one who ran off the first time I saw you?"

"Yes." Sumiko laughed. "She was scared of you."

"She seems a little scary herself. But why are you wearing lipstick?"

"That's what I asked her," Tak-Tak chimed in.

She answered, "Because it's red."

"Your lips are already red," Frank said.

"But they're a different shade of red," she said. *"Obviously."*

"Right, but—never mind." He shook his head as if to rid himself of the illogical thoughts she was trying to put into his brain.

Tak-Tak said, "She was even wearing lipstick when she was working in her garden."

Frank smiled at him. "That's strange, huh?"

"Yes."

To Sumiko, Frank said, "What kind of garden?"

"Some vegetables, a pond, and some flowers called 'stock.' They have a beautiful scent."

"They stink funny," said Tak-Tak, laughing.

Frank laughed too.

"It won third place in the camp competition," Sumiko said defensively.

"Can I see your garden?"

"What for?"

"So I can describe it to my brother. Maybe we'll have a garden with a pond too." He paused. "Maybe we'll have one in front and one in back."

"I doubt if you're allowed to walk around camp without a good reason," Sumiko said.

Tak-Tak said to Sumiko, "We could take him when everybody else is at dinner." Then he asked Frank,

"Want to play cards until then?" Frank raised his eyebrows at Sumiko before turning his attention to the cards. She didn't say anything. *Maybe* it would be all right to bring him into the camp.

While it grew darker, Tak-Tak taught Frank a *hanafuda* game he had made up. The way Tak-Tak explained it didn't make any sense, but Frank listened patiently. They both ignored Sumiko. When the dinner gongs started sounding, Tak-Tak said, "Come on!" Sumiko didn't argue.

They slipped into camp, sticking to the shadows as Tak-Tak showed Frank some of the gardens: the rock gardens; the pond gardens; the gardens with carved Buddhas, vases, and warriors; the vegetable gardens; the waterfall gardens; and, finally, Sumiko and Mr. Moto's garden. It stretched halfway across the length of the barrack. Some nights Mr. Moto took down the cheesecloth, but tonight the white cloth rippled above the plants.

"Do you like it?" Sumiko felt kind of shy to be showing him her garden. "It's hard to see how pretty the flowers are in the dark."

"I can see," he said. "It looks like . . . you."

Sumiko suddenly felt pleasure from that remark, like a tingling warmth through her whole body. *It looks like you.*

From somewhere outside the warmth, a boy called out, "An Indian! His father built the barbed-wire fence!"

The warmth turned to a chill. Sumiko saw a swarm of boys running toward Frank, the dust swirling around their pounding feet as if they were creating smoke as they ran. Frank's own feet also raised dust as he scrambled to the fence.

Sumiko shouted, "No!" But her voice got lost in the cries of the boys. She saw Frank's shirt rip as he struggled through a break in the barbed wire. Some boys had already cut a hole in the fence. She screamed "No!" again as loudly as she could. But the boys didn't seem to hear her—it was like yelling to a wave in the ocean. The boys caught Frank just outside the fence and surrounded him, pummeling him with their fists.

Sumiko found herself running before she was even fully aware that she *was* running. The fence dug into her arms as she pushed through to reach Frank. She felt the shock of wire ripping into her skin. The boys and Frank were like a big tumbleweed rolling over the desert. Sumiko screamed at them, "It wasn't his father! His father is dead!"

She grabbed one boy by the collar of his shirt and tried to pull him away, but he pushed her to the ground. "Leave him alone!" she grunted as they wrestled for a moment.

She looked around wildly and spotted a mesquite branch on the ground. She picked it up and closed her eyes and prayed for one second. Then, keeping her eyes closed, she swung the stick and felt it strike something hard. Everything was still and quiet. She opened her eyes. Blood dripped down the face of one of the boys; it was a black trickle in the night. The hurt boy looked at her, stunned. She felt kind of stunned herself. "I'm sorry," she said, but she didn't put the stick down. The boy ran off crying.

The other boys stared at Sumiko for a moment. One of them said, "You hit Kenji!" before they all ran off after their friend. They crawled through the wire and ran back into the camp.

Frank stood up, and he and Sumiko looked at each other. He was dirty, and a lump like a plum was already swelling on one of his cheeks.

"I tried to tell them," she said.

Frank didn't answer. "I'd better go. Will you be in trouble?"

"I don't know."

"He wasn't hurt bad," Frank said.

"It was bloody."

"I don't think it was bad," he said.

"But are you okay?"

"I'm fine." He seemed annoyed with her. "You don't have to protect *me*." She just stared at his bruised face. He softened. "But thank you," he said. "I mean it. So, come to the river with Bull on Saturday."

"Why all the way to the river?"

"Because I don't want to get beat up again. Eight o'clock Saturday morning. Just take the path straight to the river. We'll find you."

She realized then that Tak-Tak was standing beside her, and he held a stick too. "Did you hit anyone?" she asked.

"No, because nobody hit *you*."

He leaned against her as they watched Frank walk off into the night. She had a funny feeling then, one that didn't make any sense: Because she had protected Frank, she felt like he was now officially and definitely her friend.

26

SUMIKO CLEANED HER SCRATCHED ARM WITH THE BUCKET of water they always kept in their room. She hid her torn clothes in her suitcase under her cot. She thought she knew where the boy Kenji lived. She picked some stock for Kenji, even though most boys didn't like flowers. But it was all she had to give him.

He lived four blocks away, with his mother, father, and seven siblings. He was sitting out front with his older brothers and some friends when Sumiko walked up. The area right above his eye was cut, but not as badly as she would have thought.

"Hi," she said to him.

"Hi," he said reluctantly.

"I brought you flowers to apologize for hitting you."

One of his brothers said, "I thought you said an Indian hit you."

An older boy said, "You mean a *girl* hit you?" It was the same boy who'd started the fight at the basketball game.

Kenji didn't answer. The older boys laughed. "A girl hit him!" they teased. They walked off laughing.

Kenji glared at her. "What are you, an *inu*?"

"The *inu* spy for the *hakujin*, not the Indians."

He looked at her as if he smelled vinegar. Still, he took the flowers she handed him.

"Do you have any candy?" he asked. "If you do, we'll call it even."

"Okay, I'll owe you."

"All right. And don't tell anyone I got hit by a girl," he warned.

Sumiko could still see the older boys walking off in the distance. "It seems like everyone already knows . . . now."

"Just don't tell anyone else."

"Okay," she said.

She went home and collapsed on her cot, feeling exhausted. Auntie and Tak-Tak were already sleeping, but Bull and Ichiro weren't home yet. Many nights Ichiro stayed away until late, sometimes with a favorite girl and sometimes with his friends in the boiler room, so they could talk man talk together. Bull said Ichiro liked to talk about politics and the war. Of course, nobody got reliable war news in camp.

Once Sumiko had asked Frank for war news. At the time, he said Japan had expanded into Borneo, Java, and Sumatra. Russian forces were fighting to protect Stalingrad. The Allies were fighting Hitler's forces in North Africa. War seemed incredibly complicated.

But that all seemed far away as she lay in her cot, cold and exhausted. She fell asleep and woke in the middle of the night. Ichiro was still gone, but Bull lay in bed. Sumiko had no idea what time it was.

"Bull?" Sumiko asked. "Are you awake?"

Bull groaned a bit from his cot; obviously, he'd been asleep. "What is it?" She saw the mist from his mouth dissipate in the air.

She should have let him sleep, but instead she asked, "You won't join the army, will you, if they let you?"

No one had closed the curtains. Sumiko saw the crescent moon hanging in the window. Several bats crossed the sky.

"I don't know." He paused. "I know Ich won't join."

"Do you and Ich still like each other?"

He sighed. "Go to sleep, Sumiko."

But she felt wide awake now. She put on her shoes

and—wrapped in a blanket—ventured outside. The stars were beautiful. Even the desert looked beautiful, but lonely, as she moved through the quiet camp.

When she passed the basketball court, she saw a girl flitting in an amazing fashion across the ground. It was the girl who'd been talking to the Indian player, and she was dancing. The only light came from the moon and a dim bulb outside a latrine. The girl's feet moved across the court like pebbles skipping across water. She leaped in the air and seemed to catch a breeze as she rose. She twirled, her straight hair swirling around her head. A lot of people thought she was strange. She wanted to be a dancer, but nobody had ever seen her dance, and she never entered any of the talent contests. Watching her, Sumiko knew that the girl had been struck with a type of lightning when she was born. There were people like that in the world.

There was a movement from the shadows, and Sumiko saw an Indian boy looking right at her. He was from the basketball team. His face was happy. Sumiko smiled, and he smiled back. The girl was oblivious. Sumiko slipped away to leave them alone.

27

THE NEXT NIGHT WHILE BULL WAS OUTSIDE SMOKING, Sumiko decided to go talk to him. As she approached him she took smaller and smaller steps. She was taking tiny half steps when she noticed he was looking at her.

Bull laughed. "I keep thinking you're growing up, but . . ."

It was a cool evening in early February, but Bull wore just a short-sleeved shirt. The temperature was scarcely warmer inside than out, and Sumiko's fingers were already cold.

"Bull?"

"Unh."

"I have a friend."

"Good."

"It's an Indian friend," she said quickly, and braced for his reaction.

Bull blew a couple of smoke rings into the air, but the rings quickly broke up in the breeze. Finally he said, "A friend is a friend."

"Would you like to meet him?"

"Unh."

"He's bringing his brother to meet you."

"They sneak into camp when you meet?"

"No. They never do that. I mean, they were in camp once. I mean, one of them was. Last night, in fact. I don't know if you'd say he sneaked in exactly. We just walked in, so personally, I wouldn't use the word *sneak*."

Bull smiled slightly. "I'm glad that's settled."

"And we don't exactly meet. Sometimes he's just there."

"Hmm."

"What do you mean by 'hmm'?"

"I mean 'hmm.'" She studied his face and somehow saw that he was just teasing her. He wasn't smiling, but she could tell.

She laughed. "You're distracting me! I want to know, will you come meet them?"

"Me? If you want."

"Good! We're going to do it tomorrow morning—they're already expecting you."

"How can they be expecting me when you just asked me?"

"Because I knew you'd come! We're leaving at seven in the morning."

"All right."

Tak-Tak called her inside then. He lay bundled in bed. "I'm cold!" he said. Though the *Chronicle* had cautioned everyone to be careful with heating devices, Ichiro had made a couple of heaters out of sand placed in cans with charcoal on top. There had been a few household fires in camp already. Some were caused by homemade heaters, and some were caused by the lines people attached to the main electrical wire to get more power into their barracks. Sumiko brought one of their heaters closer and lay on Tak-Tak's cot with her arms around her brother to keep him warm.

"Sumiko?"

"Uh-huh?"

"Are we orphans?"

"You know we're not."

"'Cause my friend said I'm an orphan."

"I used to think that too," she said. "But the orphanage is in another camp, in Manzanar. If we were orphans, we'd be there."

"Sumiko?" he whispered.

"What?" she whispered back.

"Did you kill that boy yesterday?"

"No," she said, still whispering. "I saw him afterward. He didn't even need stitches."

"Was he mad at you?"

"Yes."

"Is he going to hurt you?"

"No. I said I was sorry," she said.

"Are you?"

She thought that over. "No."

"Good. Good night."

"Good night."

28

IT FELT STRANGE TO WALK DOWN THE PATH TO THE RIVER with Bull. She felt as if she were kind of a tour guide, even though she'd been to the river just once, on Christmas. "I think that big tree is about the halfway mark to the river," she told Bull.

They arrived first. Sumiko laid out a blanket she'd brought, and she and Bull sat down. She saw Bull all the time, but now she felt sort of shy, but also excited. He looked so strong! She felt proud that he was her cousin.

When Frank and his brother Joseph arrived, Joseph was smoking and Bull had just put a cigarette into his mouth and was looking for matches. Joseph handed him his cigarette to use for lighting up. Sumiko flashed a bright smile at Frank.

Sumiko thought Frank looked flustered and excited that they were all meeting. She felt the same way. He and Sumiko started talking at the same time, and then they both stopped.

Joseph extended an arm and shook hands with Bull. "Joseph," he grunted.

"Bull," Bull grunted.

Joseph gestured toward his brother. "Frank."

Bull indicated Sumiko. "Sumiko," he said.

Joseph glanced at Frank and said, "I thought her name was Weedflower." Sumiko frowned at Frank, but he ignored her.

Joseph was tall and slender, maybe a little younger than Ichiro. He seemed kind of arrogant and kind of nice—like Frank, except older. Or rather, Frank was like his brother. Sumiko noticed that Frank almost seemed to be studying Joseph.

Frank said, "Joseph is leaving soon for the army."

"I heard," said Bull.

Sumiko hit Bull's arm. "Don't tell him everything I said!" She glanced at Joseph. "Not that I said anything."

Bull just shrugged at Joseph.

Joseph studied Sumiko seriously, then suddenly seemed amused. "So you're our little enemy girl," he said. His eyes drifted down to her sweater.

It was Bull's and was about ten thousand sizes too big.

"It's Bull's," she said.

Everybody looked blankly at her. "What's Bull's?" Frank finally said.

"Oh. My sweater . . . I mean Bull's sweater."

Frank turned to Joseph. "She means she's wearing Bull's sweater," he said, as if she spoke a different language.

Sumiko and Frank met eyes, and for some reason both broke out in giggles. Bull and Joseph shrugged at each other.

"Let's sit down!" Sumiko suggested brightly.

They all sat down on the blanket. Frank seemed eager for everybody to get along. He looked attentively back and forth among all of them.

Joseph spoke directly to Bull. "When I get back, I plan to farm. I heard you're an expert farmer."

"Bull's a great farmer!" Sumiko said. "He's kind of a genius when it comes to farming."

Bull said only, "We had a small flower farm."

Joseph nodded. He started to say something, stopped to draw on his cigarette, and then said, "I don't know if you realize it, but the tribal council voted against having the camp here."

"Is that so?" Bull said. Even when he didn't make expressions, Sumiko usually knew what Bull was thinking. Now she had no idea.

"The federal government put it here anyway," Joseph said. "Why do they ask us for our opinion if they don't care what we say?"

Sumiko said tentatively, "Because it's a democracy?"

Joseph laughed, but not in a friendly way. Bull wrinkled the area between his eyes.

Sumiko felt her face grow hot. "It is a democracy," she insisted. "Everybody gets a vote."

Joseph didn't laugh this time. He met eyes with Frank.

Then Frank told her, "It's against the law for Indians to vote."

"Are you sure?" Sumiko said, and immediately felt stupid for asking. It was just that in school a long time ago the class had learned that all grown-ups born in the United States could vote.

"How come you can't vote?" Bull asked.

Joseph nodded at Frank, apparently to indicate that Frank should answer. Sumiko thought Frank looked proud that his brother wanted him to explain. "Indians were declared citizens by the U.S. government in 1924, but the states decide individually who can vote or not. Arizona doesn't allow it." Frank turned to his brother as if for approval; Joseph nodded.

"I don't want to vote anyway," Sumiko said.

There was a silence. Bull said gently, "Still, they should have the right, Sumi-chan." Sumiko lowered her head and felt her face heat up again.

She was glad when Frank changed the subject by abruptly announcing, "She eats snakes!"

Sumiko laughed. "It's tasty with ginger! You can also put *shoyu* on it or dry it and salt it. My neighbor Mr. Moto says it's very versatile. I ate it for the first time the day I arrived in camp."

Joseph made a gesture exactly like Sumiko had seen Frank make: He shook his head as if to clear out the illogic she was putting there. Now she knew where Frank had gotten the gesture. "She likes to talk," Joseph said to Frank. But he smiled when he said it. Then he turned to Bull and said, "I have some questions about the irrigation and your farm if you don't mind."

The men walked down to the river and disappeared in the reeds. Frank seemed delighted, childlike in a way Sumiko hadn't seen him before. He kept looking starry-eyed toward the river where his brother had gone. "Joseph and my other brother, Henry, are the two smartest men I know. When they come back, they're going to help make sure the whole reservation gets irrigated," he told her.

"Are you worried that they're going to get hurt?"

"Oh, no, they'll kill about a hundred Germans or Japs. . . ." His voice trailed off. "I mean, I'm not worried. They'll come back heroes." Sumiko didn't answer, and his face turned sincere and beautiful. "I'm sorry."

"I know what you meant. You meant, uh . . ."

"I meant they'll kill the enemy. . . . I mean, you're not the enemy. . . ."

They were silent for a moment. Everybody in America said "Japs"—*everybody*. Even some Japanese said it. But hearing it from Frank sounded awful.

"Is he going to the Pacific?"

"I don't know."

Then Frank looked down, his face very sad, and Sumiko knew he *was* worried about his brothers.

She tried to think of something to say. She wanted to change the subject so he wouldn't be sad. "So where do you live, anyway? Is it, you know, a regular house?"

"What do you mean?"

"I don't know. In the movies . . ." In the movies Indians had tepees. Now it was her turn to let her voice trail off.

"It's made of mud and thatch. My father built it. We just sleep in it. We cook outside."

"How do you do homework at night without electricity?"

"We have an oil lamp. But I don't have much time for homework. I cut wood for people for extra money. And I have to babysit my sister all the time. Anyway, we all go to sleep pretty early."

"How come all your names are . . . well, they're not Indian."

"I guess the government didn't want us to have Indian names."

There was a moment of silence before she said, "Well, what do you want to do someday?"

"Work for my brothers."

"What will you grow on your farm?"

He thought a moment. "Everything."

He watched her patiently, apparently waiting for the next question. When it didn't come, he asked, "Are you going to be a farmer too?"

"Before the war I wanted to own a flower shop someday, but now I don't know. I may end up working in a factory."

He spoke really softly, and really coldly. "You don't need white people to tell you it's okay to own a flower shop."

"I do now."

"No," he said. "*No.* You don't." The coldness left him then. "Do you miss your farm?"

"I did, but now I have my garden. Later this year I want to take first place in the camp competition." She paused. "A few people are leaving the camp for jobs outside. But most people aren't leaving. The jobs are really crummy. You have to apply to the administration, and they decide if they should let you go. But we're staying here." She paused, then added quietly, "Everybody hates us out there."

"It's bad for us if too many of you leave. We won't

get as much land cultivated without you," Frank said offhandedly.

She felt annoyed, because the government wanted them *out* because it was better for white people and their crops that needed picking, and the Office of Indian Affairs probably wanted them *in* because it was better for getting land cultivated.

But she had to admit that it would be bad for the Japanese to leave. "It's safer in here," she said. "If we leave and try to rebuild our lives, they'll just take everything away again if Japan starts to win the war or bombs the United States again. Next time they'll be even meaner." Frank didn't answer, but she realized she actually had more to say on the subject. "Not one person on my block is leaving. We get free food, and we have our own camp government. I think we might have more freedom in camp than we would outside right now."

Frank glanced at the reeds. She heard the wind weave through the trees and imagined it rippling the water, more and more wind, an endless supply. They both felt something in the air at the same time and stood up together to check the sky. It was getting dark: a dust storm.

They crashed through the brush by the river. Joseph and Bull were hunkered down, Bull drawing something in the dirt as Joseph watched intently. They barely glanced at Sumiko and Frank.

"Dust storm's coming," Frank called.

Joseph and Bull stood up and faced each other. They shook hands. "Thanks for meeting with me," Joseph said.

"Read that book," Bull said. "Don't forget the title: *Basic Irrigation for Small Farms* by Samuel Morrison. It was the best book I ever read."

Sumiko hadn't even known Bull had ever read a book.

Bull continued, "You can't put it down. It's better than a mystery. I read it three times."

"I'll make sure to get it."

They all walked silently to the dirt path that led to camp. Joseph shook Sumiko's hand. In all her life Sumiko had shaken hands with only two people who weren't Japanese. One was Mrs. Melrose, and the other was Joseph. "It was nice to meet you." Joseph said to Frank, "You're right. She's very pretty." Sumiko wasn't sure whether to feel pleased or embarrassed.

"Nice to meet you, Joseph," she said. "Good luck."

"See ya, Weedflower," Frank said to Sumiko.

"Bye, Woodcutter," she said.

Sumiko and Bull walked off together. The wind was getting stronger and stronger. The storm reached them when they were only halfway back. They curled on the ground next to each other, Bull with his arms around her holding the blanket down. The wind was especially harsh. But Bull's muscles bulged around Sumiko; she knew she was safe.

She kept her eyes and mouth shut tight, except for once when a gust of wind punched into her, and her mouth and eyes opened in surprise. All she could see was the blue from the blanket and the swirling dust. Bull pushed her head back down and pulled the blanket back around them. She had a crazy feeling that they were going to be lifted into the sky.

When the wind began to die down, Bull relaxed his hold, but just a little. She could tell he was reluctant to get up yet. "Do you think Frank and Joseph are okay?" Sumiko shouted over the wind.

"Yes," Bull said confidently.

"How do you know?"

"I just know."

As usual after a dust storm, the camp was desolate when they got back. Everybody was still waiting inside. There was no human movement anywhere at all. There were some stray branches here and there, but otherwise, it didn't look that different from the way it always did. It was dusty before a dust storm, and it was dusty after a dust storm.

The first person they saw emerge from the barracks was Mr. Moto. He stepped out to uncover his snake cage. Some of Sumiko's flowers were listing over, and dust and debris floated atop Mr. Moto's pond. One of the handful of dogs that lived in camp ran around barking, glad to be free again to roam. When Mr. Moto saw Sumiko, he closed his eye and squeezed, then said, "Don't worry, the garden is fine."

Everybody was at home when Bull and Sumiko walked in. Auntie was already trying to clean up the dust that now covered everything inside. In short, everything seemed perfectly normal.

29

THEN SOMETHING HAPPENED SO BIG THAT SUMIKO COULD think of nothing else.

One morning in February when Sumiko arrived at the schoolhouse, the other kids in her class were hovering around a bonfire, refusing to go inside at the start of school. It wasn't terribly cold, but it was chilly, and Sumiko knew they were all utterly sick of school.

"Come on now, let's get inside," Miss Kelly pleaded. Sumiko leaned over the fire and pretended she hadn't heard.

Miss Kelly didn't try again. In fact, Miss Kelly herself seemed seduced by the fire. Several men walked by talking loudly. "It's an outrage!" Sumiko heard one say angrily. Two women dashed by chattering in Japanese. A couple of men rushed right behind them. Sumiko could tell something big was happening, and she felt her insides twist up with worry about what this big thing was.

One of the boys in her class called out to a man, "What's going on?"

"It doesn't concern children!" the man barked at him before walking quickly past.

That made them all even more curious. "Miss Kelly, won't you ask someone what's going on?" Sumiko said.

Her classmates echoed, "Yes, Miss Kelly, ask someone!"

"I'll ask someone if you children come inside so we can start class."

The fire was warm and felt nice. But Sumiko wanted to know what was going on. "I'll come in," she said.

"Me too," Sachi said. Soon everyone else agreed.

Miss Kelly flagged down a couple of men and drew her coat tight before leaving the fire. As she talked to the men she pulled a pen and paper from her bag and wrote some things down. She took an awfully long time talking, listening, writing, and talking some more. Sumiko wondered what could be so complicated.

When Miss Kelly returned, she told the class,

"Inside, all of you! Come on, come inside and I'll tell you what's happening."

Inside, Miss Kelly stood in front of the room, still pulling her coat tightly around herself. She paused to look blankly at the class. Sumiko couldn't help smiling whenever she saw Miss Kelly's expression at the start of every day. She always looked surprised to find herself in a dirty desert classroom in front of a room full of unruly Japanese kids.

"Okay then, here it is verbatim," Miss Kelly said. She read from her notes. "'Every man or woman in camp aged seventeen or older will be required to fill out a questionnaire in preparation for instituting a military draft of young *Nisei* men.'"

"Why?" several kids shouted out.

Miss Kelly took a big breath. "I'm trying to tell you. Just listen." She looked back down at her paper.

"They'll be asked many questions, including two important ones. The first is, 'Are you willing to serve in the armed forces of the United States on combat duty, wherever ordered?' And the second is, 'Will you swear unqualified allegiance to the United States of America and faithfully defend the United States from any or all attack by foreign or domestic forces and forswear any form of allegiance to the Japanese emperor or to any other foreign government, power, or organization?'"

One boy said, "It's a trick! If my father says yes

and forswears allegiance to Japan and they don't give him rights here, we won't have any country at all!" That made sense to Sumiko.

Another boy said, "If your father *doesn't* answer yes, they might send you to Japan!" That made sense too.

Sumiko didn't know whether all this was rumor or fact. There were always a lot of rumors. One week everybody had heard that Poston would be closed and that they'd all be sent to one of the camps in Arkansas. Another week everybody heard that a man everyone trusted was an *inu*. Sometimes there were rumors of impending beatings. Sometimes there were rumors that nobody would be getting paychecks that week. And so on, a constant supply of new rumors.

Then everyone was shouting at once. Sumiko didn't know what to think of this new information. A couple of kids ran out of the barrack.

"Can we leave? It's too cold for class!" one of the girls cried out.

As an answer, Miss Kelly opened a book. She read a portion out loud and then passed it around to the students so they could read out loud. No one read with enthusiasm. Fortunately, that afternoon Miss Kelly let them out early, and Sumiko rushed away with her chair. She wanted to know what Bull and Ichiro thought of this new government information.

On the way home Sumiko passed groups of men arguing in the streets and aisles of Poston. Sometimes she just walked right up and started listening until the men made her go away. Other times she walked slowly, pretending to be struggling with her chair. In this way she learned that some people believed the questions were designed to trick them. If you agreed to forswear allegiance to Japan, wouldn't the authorities assume that you'd held such an allegiance in the first place? And then punish you somehow?

And some people wanted to know what exactly was a "foreign power or organization"? Did that mean you wouldn't be allowed to join organizations with *Issei* as members?

Other people said they would forswear allegiance to Japan only if the United States gave them back their full rights first. And the young men wondered, What if they died for their country and their families were never even given back their rights?

When Sumiko got home, she found no surprises. Auntie and Bull had already decided to answer yes to both questions, as had Mr. Moto. And Mr. Moto had insisted his son do the same. But Sumiko worried about what Ichiro would say. Nobody had seen him around that day. And Sumiko also worried about what Jiichan and Uncle would answer on their questionnaires up in their camp. It was so long ago that she had last seen them!

It seemed amazing to Sumiko that the government would round up all the Japanese, throw them in camps, and then let the men out to join the army for no other reason than that they wrote "yes-yes" to two particular questions on a form. If all it took to prove your loyalty was to fill out some form, why hadn't the government given them the form before putting them in camps?

Most of the residents of Poston quickly answered "yes-yes," and the administration announced that those who answered "no-no" would be shipped off to the camp at Tule Lake, California. Meanwhile "loyal" residents of Tule Lake—those who had answered "yes-yes" to both questions—could choose to be shipped to other camps, including Poston. And in the future Tule Lake would no longer be considered a relocation center but, rather, a segregation center. All of this based on a form people filled out! Everybody called the men being shipped to Tule Lake "No-No Boys."

Most amazingly, the government was now calling on young men to sign up for a special draft for an all-*Nisei* combat team of about five thousand men. Bull was literally first in line to sign up. And a couple of days after Bull signed up, Ichiro shocked them all by announcing that he would sign up as well. He said he was doing it for Sumiko and Tak-Tak.

"For us?" Sumiko said.

"I'm gonna kill some Nazis and get you out of here faster," Ichiro bragged. "I'm gonna get twenty medals and marry the prettiest girl I can find."

Sumiko didn't know how Frank could stand knowing that his brothers were fighting. The thought of someone shooting at Bull or Ichiro made her sick. And even though it made her sick, she couldn't stop thinking about it. At night she lay in bed and listened to the sound of their breathing and tried to imagine this room without that sound. How quiet and empty the room would be! How small their family was getting!

Some of the men who'd joined the army got married before they left. Ichiro thought about marrying one of the girls he dated, but he couldn't decide which one, so then he figured that if he couldn't decide, maybe it was a sign that he shouldn't get married.

Some nights Sumiko felt too sad to be inside listening to everyone breathe. Tak-Tak's nose was often stuffed, and Sumiko hated to listen to him struggle for breath. She imagined his lungs brown from dust. And Auntie was so depressed about Bull and Ichiro leaving that she cried for hours at night. Sumiko thought there was nothing in the world sadder than listening to someone cry for hours. It was even worse than your own tears.

So Sumiko would wrap herself in a blanket and

take her chair outside to sit in the desert. The dry winds often kept the world around her in constant motion. One night two huge white clouds stretched out on either side of the moon. It looked like a giant moth, with the moon as the moth's body and the clouds as glowing wings. The beautiful white moth took up half the sky.

Sumiko remembered what Frank had said about your ancestors watching you, and she thought maybe the moth in the sky might be her mother watching her. She wished she could ask Frank about it. She wished she had a telephone. She didn't know his phone number, though, or even if he had a phone. She had never actually used a telephone, but it looked easy enough.

The wings of the moth began to spread across the sky.

If that was her mother in the sky, what was it that her mother wanted to tell her?

She remembered the summer nights when she'd slept out here and looked at the stars. She'd tried to go back in time, first to before her birth and then to when her parents were getting married, with her mother in the kimono that Jiichan said had made her look like a flower. And then she would go back before that to when Jiichan had come on the boat from Japan. And then she would skip way back to the time of the samurai. And then she would fall asleep.

Now her mind went back to before she was born and her parents had first fallen in love. Jiichan had once said that he had never seen anything like it, the way they loved each other. Sumiko liked to imagine it. She knew what they looked like because of the photograph that used to sit on the dining-room bureau. Even now she could picture them easily. So she realized it didn't matter that the photograph had been burned, because she could see it clearly in her head. And that was what Sumiko was thinking of when she fell asleep in the chair.

30

THE FIELDS HAD GROWN BARE OVER THE WINTER.

The *Poston Chronicle* said that in the spring the internees from Poston would plant twenty acres of cantaloupes, ten acres of tomatoes, five acres of squash, five acres of chard, three acres of cucumbers, ten acres of Hubbard squash, twelve acres of daikon, twelve acres of beans, two acres of okra, ten acres of corn, four acres of eggplant, and twenty acres of sweet potatoes. The camp took up seventy-one thousand acres, and the great majority of *Nikkei* were farmers. And they were not even growing enough to feed themselves. Still, it was a start.

After Bull and Joseph met, Sumiko walked

through the brush nearby every day, but Frank never showed up. At first she thought he was just really busy cutting wood. But when day after day he never showed up, she started to feel angry and betrayed. He'd probably been using her just so Joseph could meet Bull. That would mean he hadn't been her friend after all!

Every time she visited the empty brush fields, she walked dejectedly back. Camp had started to seem different lately, not so permanent anymore. More and more young men were joining the army, and a couple of people on her block had actually decided to leave camp for outside jobs in a candy factory.

Sumiko generally didn't give much thought to the government's attempts to get them out of the camps because so few people were leaving. The departures were more of a trickle than a stream. One man who'd left camp for a while came back and warned couples with babies to be careful about where they went if they left camp. He said that some whites were still so angry about Pearl Harbor, they wanted to kill Japanese babies.

Sumiko asked Mr. Moto if he still planned to stay, and he said, "Yes, oh, yes. I'm too tired out from everything that's happened. I don't have the strength to go through all that now."

Sumiko knew that without Uncle, Jiichan, or one of her sons, Auntie would never leave camp.

Plus, Auntie, whose previous life had been work and only work, enjoyed her sewing club. So Sumiko was shocked—actually, truly shocked—when Auntie sat everybody down one day and announced that she had gotten permission for them to leave camp.

"I've found a job in a sewing factory near Chicago."

"But, Auntie!" was all Sumiko could think of to say at first. "Auntie, we're safe here!" she added.

"We have to leave at some point. Now is best."

"Why is now best? We should wait for the end of the war! What about my garden? I'm going to win first prize this year."

Bull said gently, "Sumiko, what if the war lasts ten years?"

"Bull, they'll put us right back in here if Japan bombs Hawaii again."

"I'm not going unless Sumiko goes," said Tak-Tak, throwing his arms around his sister.

Everybody looked at her. "Why can't Tak-Tak and I stay with Uncle Kenzo? He's as much my relative as you are!"

Everybody was surprised, and Auntie looked hurt. Sumiko hadn't seen Uncle Kenzo since his birthday, when Auntie had made her visit him. Sumiko tried to keep her expression firm.

Finally Auntie said, "Don't be silly," and she left it at that.

Later Sachi told Sumiko, "I wouldn't go if I were

you. The *hakujin* will hang your brother from a tree."

The scary thing was that it was easy for Sumiko to picture her little brother hanging from a tree.

All throughout camp the no-no commotion continued. One afternoon Sumiko was pulling weeds from the garden when dozens of No-No Boys marched past her waving Japanese flags and shouting. One of them called out to her, "Join us, little girl!" and the men around him laughed as they all marched on. She got up and watched them as they rounded the corner and then proceeded up the long side of camp. A part of her did want to join them.

The government moved her people around like they were animals. And yet as Sumiko walked through camp she was struck by how familiar it all seemed, while her old life on the farm seemed unreal. When camp was dry, the inescapable dust seemed familiar; and when camp was wet, the inescapable mud seemed familiar.

When she got home, she found some neighbors shouting at each other.

"The government wants to tell us where we can live or not live once we get outside!" one shouted. "I'm staying right here!"

Another man shouted back, "Look, we need to move out to prove to them we can be trusted outside."

"Why do we have to prove anything to them?" the other man screamed.

The first man grew suddenly solemn as he said, "Because we have no choice."

Sumiko had read a letter that Mr. Moto's nephew had written him from outside. The nephew said that he and other *Nikkei* didn't like to be seen together in public—*hakujin* got nervous when they saw Japanese in groups. Sumiko got a new letter also. Auntie must have written Jiichan that Sumiko wanted to stay in camp, because the latest letter she received from him exhorted her to leave: *I know nobody care about old man opinion, but I say you leave camp.*

The grown-ups could debate all they wanted. *She* would find a way to stay. It wasn't so bad here any-more. There were parties and dances and movies and free meals. And she had her garden and three friends. Trees and flowers grew on every block. Together the Japanese had made the desert bloom. Even the white men thought so. Even the Indians thought so. Every-body thought so.

Bull started sleeping outside although the weather was still cool at night. He wanted to be alone all the time now. Sumiko would stand at the door and see his big form rising and falling on the cot as he breathed. She tried to imagine what kind of girl he would marry someday. No doubt a hardworking one. He would probably end up in an arranged marriage. He would love his wife, though, because that's the way he was.

For some reason, watching him out there one night, Sumiko thought of the canoe he and Ichiro had built when Bull was fourteen and Ichiro eighteen. They'd built it for her seventh birthday, when she was still crying all the time about her parents' death. They'd painted the canoe blue, and when it rained hard and the long, sloping road nearby flooded, her cousins took her and baby Tak-Tak out in the boat and they drifted downhill for miles, surrounded by soaking flower farms. Sumiko remembered that Bull smiled as he saw her laughing and that she'd known right then she still had a family.

31

THE LAST OF THE NO-NO BOYS WERE SHIPPED TO TULE Lake, while some yes-yes families were transferred from Tule Lake to Poston. The camp changed after that. There were no more beatings. There were fewer arguments. All anybody thought of were the men who'd volunteered for the army. Waiting for Bull and Ichiro to leave for basic training was worse even than the waiting after Pearl Harbor.

Dozens of young men were shipping out soon. On many nights all across camp you could hear the good-bye parties or see the future soldiers with their girl-friends or wives crying in their arms.

Auntie scarcely paid attention to Sumiko. One

day Sumiko decided to take the bus to Camp One to visit her Uncle Kenzo and ask him whether she and Tak-Tak could live with his family.

Looking at her camp from the bus, she was impressed and proud of how beautiful it had become. There were a couple of white administration types on the bus, and they were impressed too.

"I never saw such beautiful gardens," said one.

Camp One was so big and had changed so much since Sumiko's last visit that she nearly got lost. But she found Uncle Kenzo's place again. He was sitting with some men, playing poker. As she hadn't visited since his birthday, he was surprised to see her. He certainly didn't look particularly happy at the sight.

"What is it, Sumiko?" he said. He didn't even set his cards down.

"Can I talk to you?"

"We're in the middle of a hand."

The other men stirred. "Are we playing cards or not?" one man said.

Sumiko decided to ask Uncle Kenzo her question right then and there. "Can my brother and I live with you? Auntie is going to leave camp for a job."

Uncle Kenzo frowned and finally set down his cards.

Sumiko quickly lied, "She says it's okay with her if it's okay with you."

He picked up his cards again. "The kids are going crazy in these camps. Go with your auntie, where you belong."

The other men chuckled. Sumiko felt pretty stupid as she walked out the door. On the bus ride home she felt like she was an orphan after all.

Instead of going to her barrack, Sumiko headed for the brush where she'd met with Frank and just sat outside until the sun set and she was too thirsty to stay out any longer.

A couple of days later at the good-bye party for her cousins and several others, friends of those who were leaving gave speeches about courage and strength. Sumiko just stood with her family. They hadn't spent time together in public like this in a long while. It was as if they had become a family again so that they could say good-bye properly.

Couples began to dance to a phonograph record. The weather was already warming up at night, and the room took on a sweaty smell. Ichiro danced with one of his favorite girls. Even when there was no music, they held each other and swayed as if the music were still playing. Then a reverend announced a surprise: A couple of the men would be getting married that night. Everybody cheered. Sumiko searched out Ichiro in the crowd, wondering whether he would be getting married. But two men she hardly knew made their way to the front with their future wives. The weddings took just a few minutes.

Sumiko noticed Bull leaving the party. She followed him, finding him standing near the fence outside. She stood next to him and stared out at the wild shapes of the mesquite trees.

"Will you write me?" she asked.

"Of course I will. Once a week." He looked down at her. "Sumiko, do you really want to stay here?"

"Yes."

He lit a cigarette and blew smoke over the barbed wire.

"Bull? What do you think about?"

"What do you mean?"

"I don't know. When you're walking, or just sitting, or working, or before you go to bed at night."

"Sometimes I think about the farm," he said. "I wonder who works it now and who's taking care of your *kusabana*." He smiled at her.

Sumiko thought it was sad that today there were things about the flower farm that Bull didn't know. "How long do you think the war will last?"

"I don't even know who's winning," he said.

Sumiko suddenly had a wild thought. "Someday if you have a baby, can I pick out the name?"

"I'll have to see what my wife thinks about that. But maybe."

The party inside grew quiet suddenly, one of those random silent moments that can happen in a room. A strange fear washed over Sumiko, a fear she'd never felt about Ichiro. It was a fear that Bull would not be returning. She tried to imagine him as an old man, and she could not. With Ichiro, she could see him in her mind growing older, raising the kids she knew he would have. She could see the wrinkles forming on his face. She saw the dapper old-man clothes he would wear. But with Bull, she could imagine him in his uniform but nothing beyond that. She shook off the thought.

"I'll write you all the time," she said. "Do you want magazines?"

"Don't waste your money on me."

"It won't be wasted!" she cried.

He smiled one of his rare big smiles and pulled her close against his wide chest. "Sumi-chan," he said quietly. He squeezed her so tightly that she couldn't breathe. He loosened his grip.

"I'll send you lots of magazines!" she said.

The party started to disperse. Auntie exited arm in arm with Ichiro. Bull joined them, and the three of them walked off together.

That night Bull slept outside by himself again because he said he wanted it that way. From the doorway, as Sumiko watched him lying in his cot, she hoped he was thinking about the *kusabana* blowing beneath a Southern California breeze, the scent wafting over the fields and into their home. Maybe the smell from her little garden here in camp was what had reminded him of their farm. It was April, her favorite month on the farm, full of promise and lukewarm winds.

In the morning nobody woke Sumiko up. She opened her eyes and saw Tak-Tak asleep in his cot, with his glasses on. That was her fault. She usually took them off for him at night, but she'd forgotten yesterday. She turned to check the light outlining the curtains: It looked to be about seven o'clock. She shot up, completely awake. Bull's and Ichiro's cots were gone! Auntie was folding sheets, weeping.

"Did they leave?" Stupid question, but she had to ask. Before Auntie could answer, Sumiko ran to the door and saw that the sun was already white. They'd said they were leaving at dawn. "Why didn't you wake me up?" she screamed.

Auntie didn't reply, just kept folding sheets, lovingly, even holding the sheets to her face at times to smell them. Sumiko ran out to see the road. A truck was driving by spraying water, to prevent dust from flying around later that day. There were no other vehicles in sight. She knew her cousins were long gone.

She walked back to her barrack and noticed some

papers on her pillow. They were notes from Bull about farming, to give to Frank for Joseph. Auntie had put the sheets away and was packing the tablecloth, already preparing for the move to Illinois in three weeks.

32

Every day Sumiko told her aunt that she was not leaving, and Auntie just said, "Don't be silly." Sumiko did not even begin to pack. Also, every day for the next week and a half Sumiko went to search for Frank with Bull's papers, but Frank never showed up. The corn was already tall, and the bean plants were thriving. She felt as lonely as she used to before camp. One day she actually fell asleep in a bean tunnel. She awoke to see Frank sitting a couple of feet away, just watching her. Of course she had forgotten the papers that day!

"What are you doing?" she said.

"Listening to you snore."

"Ha-ha." But he didn't smile. "I thought you had abandoned me."

He looked insulted. "Why would I do that?"

"Well, where have you been?" she asked.

"Mourning."

"Morning?"

"M-o-u-r-n-i-n-g."

"Oh . . . who . . . ," she said. She watched while he coolly blew a bubble and popped it as she waited for an answer. Then his eyes seemed to grow completely black, and very sad.

"My brother Henry," he finally said. He lay on his back and stared upward. "He was killed in battle . . . in the Pacific. We already got his remains back."

"I'm sorry!" If Henry was killed in the Pacific, that meant he was killed by Japanese soldiers. She felt guilty as if his death were her fault; and she felt defensive, in case he really thought it *was* her fault.

She lay beside him, and together they gazed through the leaves at the sky. Just when she'd decided he wasn't going to talk about it, he said, "Mohave funerals last all night. They sing the old songs for hours." He spoke as if dreaming. "We cremate the body."

"So do we," Sumiko said. "What are the songs about?"

"About the land and the river and the beginning." He suddenly turned toward her and touched her face. "How come you're still here?"

"What do you mean?"

"I thought you said some people were leaving."

"My aunt is going to get a job in Chicago. I don't want to go. Auntie may let me stay."

He didn't speak for a long time, and she saw a few tears trickling down his face. Then he said, "I'm sorry."

"For what?"

"For saying it was better for the Indians if more Japanese stayed. I was wrong."

"But you'll get more land cultivated."

"It doesn't matter. The more people who are free in the world, the better it is for Indians. It's better for everyone. You should leave. You shouldn't live here."

"*You* live here."

"My future is here," he said impatiently. "Yours is somewhere else."

Tears still fell slowly down his temple and into his hair. He wasn't crying explosively the way she had after the birthday party. So very long ago she had cried over a stupid birthday party! And he was crying because his brother was dead.

He turned to her. "So you're leaving, aren't you?"

"I don't want to. Anyway, you're my friend, right? So you should want me to stay."

"You don't know much about friendship, do you?"

"I've had friends before," she lied.

"Then you should know I'm trying to help you."

"I didn't ask for your help!"

He pushed himself up suddenly. He looked annoyed. "I'm going home." He scrambled out of the vines, leaving her lying on her back alone.

She sat up. Now *she* was annoyed. She pushed through the vines. "Frank!" she called out. But he was gone. It didn't matter; she did not know what she had planned to say to him. She lay back down and tried to figure things out.

1. She felt annoyed with Frank for wanting her to leave.
2. She felt terrible about his brother.
3. She felt responsible for his brother because he was killed by a Japanese soldier.
4. She felt worried about her cousins.
5. She felt torn about what she should do. Stay or leave?

33

At home later Sumiko borrowed Mr. Moto's shovel and started digging on the edge of her garden to extend it. The dirt was so hard, she made slow progress. She kept working even after the sun rose and the May afternoon grew sweltering. Sometimes her feelings were all jumbled together into one huge mess of sadness and fear, and sometimes her thoughts became orderly and she studied each thought in turn. And sometimes she was only gardening, only thinking of all the flowers she would grow that year.

She planned to cultivate up and down the entire length of the barrack. Maybe Mr. Moto would agree to extend the pond, and maybe they could get a tree somehow. Maybe she could live with Mr. Moto! Or maybe she could hide in the boiler room while the bus left with Auntie.

Her palms grew blistered, and she did not even eat dinner that evening, just worked and worked, though she could scarcely see in the dark.

When she finally stopped, she leaned the shovel against the barrack and sat down among her weed-flowers.

If she left the camp, she would not have any friends at all. No more Frank. No more Sachi. No more Mr. Moto. A flock of snowy egrets flew low over the ground beyond. She didn't know what to do. If she left camp, it would be just exactly as if all the years Jiichan had worked and all the years her parents had worked and all the years her aunt and uncle and cousins had worked were gone; they'd be starting all over again to make their way in a hostile land, just as Jiichan once had. And yet Jiichan had found a type of success. She realized suddenly that he had been a happy man. And a brave one.

She spotted a weed and jumped up and pulled it out. Then she saw another one and yanked that out.

She kept thinking of Jiichan on the ship to America, desperately trying to avoid the ultimate boredom. When he got here, all he'd known was hard work. What kind of freedom was that? Then she thought of what Frank had said, about his future being here and hers being elsewhere. And she realized that it had not been freedom that Jiichan came to America for, but the future. And not his future, but *hers*—the future of his unborn grandchild. *That's* why he had left Japan. He had loved her even before she was born.

"All right, I'll leave," Sumiko said suddenly. But there was nobody around to hear her decision.

That evening Sumiko sat in the bean fields for several hours, waiting for Frank to show up so she could tell him good-bye. He never did show up, but the next day she went out there again. And the next and the next and the next.

One day as Mr. Moto was planting new cuttings, she moseyed up to him.

"Hi," she said.

"Hi." He stopped working.

She shifted her weight from one foot to the other and back again. "Ummm." Her gaze moved to the best carving in the garden: a samurai so realistic, he looked like Issoumbochi, the miniature man of Japanese fairy tales. You wouldn't think a man with one eye could carve like that. "See . . . um . . . I have a friend."

Mr. Moto nodded as if he understood.

"*Annnd*, I was wanting to give my friend a special present before I leave."

"Ahhh." Now he definitely understood. "So you're

leaving after all." He grunted as he lifted himself from the ground and walked over to the samurai. Then he looked thoughtful. "But do you think the garden will be able to win a prize without this?"

Sumiko tried to think of the most truthful answer. "Yes, but it might be harder. That's why the samurai is so special. But the most important part of a garden is the things that live and die."

"Oh! A gardening philosopher!" Mr. Moto said, laughing. "Here, then. For your friend." He placed the samurai gently in her hands. "For *my* friend, to do with as she wishes."

Sumiko resisted a ridiculous urge she felt to curtsy. "But I haven't got anything for you."

"You've helped me create the next first-place garden," he said.

Frank didn't show up again that day, and finally she left a box in the tunnel. In the box were the papers from Bull, the samurai statue, and a note telling Frank what time she would be leaving in three days.

Those final days passed quickly. Sumiko talked Auntie into giving her enough money for a candy bar at the canteen, and she gave it to Kenji. So that obligation was taken care of. When the morning of their departure came, the glare from the sun was so intense that Sumiko could hardly keep her eyes open. It was the hottest day so far that year. Mr. Moto helped the family load their things on the bus. But there was no sign of Frank.

At least Sachi was there. "You're my second-best friend, next to Jeannie," Sachi said. "I wish you were staying. My parents think your family is crazy to leave."

"Maybe," Sumiko said. "I can't say yet."

"Someday when I get out, I'm going to dig up some money I buried before camp."

It was possible. Sumiko knew that some people had buried things. "All I buried was a knife," she said, thinking about her knife for the first time in months.

"I buried seven thousand dollars."

And for the first time Sumiko noticed some things in Sachi's eyes. Sadness. Fear. Loneliness. And then Sumiko knew. That was why Sachi lied.

Miss Kelly walked up suddenly.

"Hi!" Sumiko said, surprised. Miss Kelly just smiled. "Will you be staying, Miss Kelly?"

Miss Kelly nodded. "Until the war ends." She shook hands with Sumiko.

People began to board the bus. Tak-Tak walked up with his crickets slung over his shoulder. Sumiko started to step up the stairs, but she stopped. "Go on up, Tak-Tak," she said. "Save me a seat."

She walked back to Mr. Moto. "Do you know you have to get new cheesecloth every year?"

"Yes, I've already ordered more."

"Oh. Okay," she said. She turned to go, then paused and turned back to Mr. Moto. "Well, do you remember how to collect the seeds? Because my uncle developed that strain of stock, and if you don't save the seeds, the strain will die out and my uncle's work will be wasted. I've brought some of the seeds with me, but you have to keep it going too." She believed these seeds could literally be the future of stock in America. That sounded conceited, but she decided she had to say it out loud. "Those seeds may be the future of stock in America!"

He nodded, smiling a bit. "I remember everything you've told me. I had the best teacher in the world." He patted her head fondly.

"I guess that's it, then," she said. He stuck out his hand and shook hers in that aggressive way he had. Suddenly he seemed to have a tear in his eye, and he hugged her. "I always wanted a daughter!" he said.

She took a last good look at the camp, at the violet-tinged mountains in the distance, and at the darkness moving quickly toward camp. A dust storm. Then she saw something else on the horizon, a small form growing larger, kind of like when she had arrived and she had seen the man on a horse. Even before she could actually make out what it was, she knew: It was a boy on a bicycle. She ran toward the bicycle.

The bus driver called out, "Hey, where you going?"

"Just a second!" she called back.

Several people hollered out at her to hurry. "Come on. We'll miss the train in Parker!" one woman called.

The driver yelled, "Get on the bus or we'll leave without you." Sumiko knew that wasn't true and kept running toward Frank.

When Frank rode up, he was exhausted. He dropped his bicycle and hurried over. "Sorry I'm late," he said. "I brought you something. It belonged to my mother. She said I could give it to you." It was a bracelet, silver and lacy. He put it on her gently, as if her wrist were something precious like a baby bird or a newborn pup.

"I can still stay," she said, but even as she said it she knew she couldn't stay and she knew he didn't want her to. He looked gaunt and sad.

"I won't have time anymore to see you, anyway." His voice broke momentarily. "I'm the man of the house for now."

He slipped a scrap of paper into one of her hands. "Here's my address. If you write me, I'll try to write back."

"I'll write you!"

He seemed older and much lonelier than he had just a few weeks ago. He did not seem like a young boy anymore.

"All right, that's it!" called the bus driver. He made as if to close the door.

Frank smiled, but weakly. "Bye, Weedflower."

She threw her arms around his neck, and they hugged tightly.

Auntie and Tak-Tak started calling to her from the windows.

She rushed onto the bus but stopped on the steps to shout. "Hurry or you'll get caught in the dust storm!"

Frank nodded. She ran to the seat in front of Auntie and watched him from her window. He wasn't hurrying! She opened the window and shouted, "Hurry!"

As the bus drove off she could see him waiting with his bicycle, staring at her. The bus picked up speed. She leaned far out her window, calling, "Hurry! Hurry!" She screamed, *"Hurry!"*

The dust descended on the bus, and she needed to close her window. After a short time the tires got stuck and the bus stopped. She looked back toward the camp, half hidden by the swirls of dust. The world outside seemed drained of color, like a brown-and-white photograph. For a moment there was a hole in the swirls, and she thought she saw Frank huddled under a blanket. He looked so small.

She opened up the paper he'd handed her. It was damp with her perspiration, but she could still read it.

He *did* have an Indian name that just his family called him. The name was Huulas, which meant "lightning." His last name was Butler.

She started crying. "He didn't hurry," she said.

Auntie reached over the seat to pat her shoulder. "He'll be fine," Auntie said.

"He won't."

"He's a smart boy."

"How do you know?"

"Because he came to see my little silly." Sumiko was so surprised to hear Auntie call her "my little silly" in an affectionate tone that she stopped crying for a moment. Auntie did not like to show affection. Auntie suddenly blurted, "Thank you for the six dollars you set on the table for Uncle and Jiichan!" Sumiko was flabbergasted—she'd given the money so long ago. Then the moment passed, and Auntie settled back and sat stiffly in her seat. Sumiko leaned her nose against the window.

"I'm going to write Frank and Bull once a week," said Sumiko. "I have to write to Frank, Bull, Ichiro, Jiichan, and Uncle. And Mr. Moto. Four relatives, two friends." She thought about Sachi and her lying ways. "And Sachi. Even if she lies, she's my friend." The bus lurched forward suddenly. Sumiko kept watching for another opening in the storm, but none came. When the storm finally died down, she was too far from the camp to see anything—except for a lot of bright green, growing in the middle of the desert.

This is what it felt like to be leaving camp:

1. Like you didn't know if people would let you into their grocery store.
2. Like you were a pioneer in the country you were born in.
3. Like you didn't know if you would ever see your cousins again.
4. Like you had lost a friend.
5. Like maybe you might own a flower shop . . . someday.

End Note

THE 442ND REGIMENTAL COMBAT TEAM, COMPOSED mostly of Japanese Americans, went on to become one of the most decorated combat units in American history. They're a legend among Japanese Americans today. In what were known as reverse AWOLs, wounded 442nd soldiers began to escape from hospitals to return to combat. While many of their families remained imprisoned, the members of the 442nd suffered what many experts agree was a 300 percent casualty rate.

During World War II, thousands of Indians left their reservations for the first time to serve in the armed forces or work at war-related jobs. It was the biggest single-event exodus from tribal lands in American history. According to John Collier, then Commissioner of Indian Affairs, if all Americans had volunteered for the military at the same rate as American Indians, there would have been no need for the Selective Service.

At war's end, as the last *Nikkei* internees were vacating Poston, Hopi from another reservation began moving into the barracks. Japanese and Hopi lived together briefly in the camp. Unused barracks were sold locally for fifty dollars apiece, mostly for residents of the reservation to use for building themselves better homes. Arizona granted Native Americans the right to vote in 1948.

Today the Poston area is rich farmland.

Here's a sneak peek at Newbery Medal-winning author Cynthia Kadohata's next novel

A MILLION SHADES OF GRAY

Available January 2010 from Atheneum Books for Young Readers

1973, Central Highlands, South Vietnam

Y'Tin Eban watched Tomas fasten the rope around Lady's neck. Lady was the smallest of the village's three elephants, but she was also the strongest, so she was much in demand as a worker. Today Lady would be dragging logs for the Buonya clan. The Buonya's house had caught fire and they were building a new one.

Tin stood behind and to the side of Tomas. Sometimes Tomas got annoyed by how closely Tin stood, but Tin didn't want to miss anything. On the other hand, Tin didn't want to annoy Tomas too much, or he might refuse to train Tin further. At fourteen, Tomas Knul was the youngest elephant handler ever in the village, but Tin hoped to beat that record. Tin was only eleven, but he was confident that he would someday be a fine elephant handler.

"Stand back," Tomas snapped. "Or I won't let you work with the elephants today."

Tin dutifully stepped back. He did whatever Tomas told him to do. There were other kids who hung around the elephants, but Tin was the one Tomas had chosen to train. Tomas had assured him that when the time was right,

Tin would become Lady's handler. Tin didn't want him to change his mind.

One of the kids who hung around got too close, and Tin snapped, "Stand back," just as Tomas had snapped to him.

Tomas glanced at Tin. "I was thinking I'd let you ride her into the village today. I'll walk beside you. Do you think you're ready?"

"I'm ready," Tin said. He had been ready for months. He patted Lady's side; she ignored him.

Tomas looked at him thoughtfully. "I think you want to be an elephant handler even more than I once did."

"Sure thing," Tin said in English. He had learned that from one of the American Special Forces soldiers with whom his father worked. The Americans had many words for "yes." "Sure," "okay," "right," "affirmative," "absolutely," "yeah," "check," "Roger that," and "Sure do, tennis shoe" immediately came to mind.

Tin walked around to Lady's trunk to have a talk with her. "I'm going to ride you in today, Lady. You need to behave yourself."

As if in answer, Lady pushed Tin to the ground—and she didn't let him up. It was embarrassing. He tried to get away, but Lady was too strong. "Tomas," he said. "Uh, can you help me?"

Tomas rolled his eyes. "Lady!" he said sharply, and Lady let Tin up. "You've got to be firmer than that," Tomas scolded Tin. "Use your hook to keep her in line."

"But I want her to like me."

"You want her to respect you. Now help get those logs

attached to her rope." Tin and one of the Buonya boys tied huge logs to the end of the rope wrapped around Lady's neck. She would haul the logs to the building site.

When the logs were secure, Tin said, "Muak, Lady." But she refused to kneel. "Muak!" He noticed Tomas looking at him. "Muak!" he said again. Tin could feel his face growing hot. He took his stick with the hook and poked her with it. She still didn't respond.

"Lady, muak," Tomas said mildly, and she immediately kneeled.

Tin climbed aboard her, his legs straddling her back. "Lady, up," Tin commanded, and for once she listened.

"Lady, han," Tomas said, and she calmly followed him, dragging the three huge logs behind her.

Tin felt a rush of happiness. When they reached the gate to the village, he sat up with his chest sticking out proudly. Lady followed Tomas to the site where the new longhouse would be built. The Buonyas were one of the biggest clans in the village, so they were planning a house that would be one hundred meters long. That translated to a lot of logs.

And so it went for the rest of the afternoon, with Lady and Tin going back and forth from the jungle to the site. At one point Lady actually kneeled when he told her to. It was just about the best day of Tin's life.

That night, as he lay in his family's room in the clan's longhouse, the others slept while he stayed up going over and over the whole afternoon. He could see Lady clearly when he closed his eyes. He felt giddy. Everyone kept saying that he was too young to know what his future held, but he knew as well as he knew anything that he would spend his life as an elephant handler. Still, his father had told him to always think about "the other hand." So, on the other hand, he had been working with Lady for five months now, and he didn't seem to be making much headway with her. When she kneeled and stood up on command today was the first time she had ever listened to him.

Tomas always warned him not to become too friendly with her or she wouldn't respect him. He liked to remind Tin of the time a few years ago when Lady went into a rage for some mysterious reason. Tin still remembered the huge gap in the fence that she had stampeded.

His father slept fitfully, mumbling about the Americans. His father had a lot on his mind lately. He worked with the American Special Forces, and had been talking to Tin's mother about the possibility of becoming a Christian. He hadn't made any decisions about it yet. He often took a long time to make a decision. For instance, it had taken him seven months to allow Tin to work with the elephants, and it had taken him two years to decide to work with the Americans.

So far the remoteness of the village had saved it from the worst of what the Americans called the Vietnam War and what his father called the American War. Tin hoped the war would be over by the time he was grown. North and South Vietnam had been fighting since well before Tin was born. The Americans fought with the South.

All his father thought about was the war, and all Tin

thought about was elephants. Tin knew he was different from the other boys in that he did not want to be a farmer. That's why his parents worried about him so much. There was just one thing he wanted: to be an elephant handler. Meanwhile Tin did so poorly in school, his parents were disappointed in him. His older sister, H'Juaih, got the highest marks. He was proud of her, but that didn't mean he wanted to be like her.

"Tin?" his mother called out from the darkness.

"Yes, Ami."

"I knew you were still awake."

And indeed she often did know when he was awake, although he didn't make a sound. He never knew whether she was awake or sleeping. Either way she was silent.

"Are you daydreaming again?"

He didn't answer.

"If you spent as much time on your homework as you do on your daydreaming, your grades would be the same as Juaih's."

"Ami, I was just thinking. That's different from daydreaming."

"How is it different?" his mother responded.

"Daydreaming is thinking about things that aren't true yet. Thinking is when you ponder matters that are already true."

She didn't answer, and he knew he had won the argument. On the other hand, maybe she just stopped talking because she was tired. He was tired also. He closed his eyes and watched Lady until he fell asleep.